IRÈNE NÉMIROVSKY

The Dogs and the Wolves

TRANSLATED FROM THE FRENCH BY
Sandra Smith

VINTAGE BOOKS
London

Published by Vintage 2010

2 4 6 8 10 9 7 5 3 1

First published in France as *Les Chiens et les Loups* by
Éditions Albin Michel in 1940
First published in Great Britain by Chatto & Windus in 2009

Vintage
Random House, 20 Vauxhall Bridge Road,
London SW1V 2SA

www.vintage-books.co.uk

Addresses for companies within The Random House Group Limited
can be found at: www.randomhouse.co.uk/offices.htm

The Random House Group Limited Reg. No. 954009

A CIP catalogue record for this book
is available from the British Library

ISBN 9780099507789

Th
Stev
cert
Gree   ).

TRANSLATOR'S NOTE

The Dogs and the Wolves was originally published in French in 1940 as *Les Chiens et les Loups*. As with many of Irène Némirovsky's titles, its translation was problematic for it evokes a particular expression in French. '*Entre chien et loup*' means 'dusk': the time of day when it is difficult to distinguish clearly between similar shapes. Simultaneously, dogs and wolves are members of the same family: the ones domesticated, the others, savage. Though the subtlety of the French expression is lost in English, the recurring theme remains clear.

Throughout the work, Némirovsky also uses variations on the word '*étrange*'. In French, this word has several connotations: 'strange', 'foreign', 'different', and, as a noun, 'outsider' as well. As a translator, it is necessary – though frustrating! – to choose one meaning. Readers should therefore keep in mind the many implications when these words arise.

The novel opens in a Ukranian city that is home to two distantly related Jewish families: the Sinners. The wealthy Sinners live high up on the hill, while their poor relations are confined to the worst part of town, down near the river. The novel follows the two sides of the family as they move to Paris, where their destinies become more and more entwined. As with many of Némirovsky's works, *The Dogs and the Wolves* explores the intricate social problems foreigners faced in 1930s France as they try to assimilate. In addition, Némirovsky provides great insight into the complex relationship between the different social classes within Jewish society itself.

The use of the family name 'Sinner' is also striking, particularly given the fact that Némirovsky had excellent English. When I asked her daughter, Denise Epstein, if she felt the choice of name was significant, she replied that she thought it had been chosen deliberately. Throughout the novel, Némirovsky plays on the concept of sin by forcing her characters constantly to make moral choices.

The Dogs and the Wolves is an important novel. It combines Némirovsky's lyrical prose with a perceptive exploration of Russian history, French society between the two world wars, immigration and religion, against the backdrop of passionate love.

Sandra Smith, Fellow
Robinson College, Cambridge
April 2009

1

The Ukrainian city in which generations of the Sinner family had been born was, in the eyes of the Jews who lived there, made up of three distinct regions. It was like a Medieval painting: the damned were at the bottom, trapped among the shadows and flames of Hell; the mortals were in the middle, lit by a faint, peaceful light; and at the top was the realm of the blessed.

In the lower part of town, down by the river, lived the scum. These were the unsavoury Jews, the self-employed craftsmen, the tenants of sordid little shops, the vagabonds, the people whose children rolled in the mud, spoke only Yiddish and wore ragged clothes with enormous caps perched above their frail necks and long dark curls. Far, far away, where lime trees crowned the tops of the hills, and important Russian officials and members of the Polish nobility had their houses, were a few beautiful villas owned by wealthy Jews. They had chosen this location because of its clean air, but most importantly because in Russia, at the beginning of the century under the reign of Nicholas II, Jews were tolerated only in certain towns, certain districts, certain streets, and sometimes only on one side of the street; the other side was out of bounds. Such restrictions, however, applied only to the poor: it was unheard of for a bribe not to circumvent even the most severe laws. It was therefore a point of honour amongst the Jews to defy them, not out of any sense of insolence or pride, but to send a message to other Jews: to show that they were worth more, had earned more money, got a better deal for their beets or corn. It was a convenient way of demonstrating wealth. So and so was born in the ghetto. By the time he was twenty, he'd made a bit of money so he could climb a rung of the social ladder; he moved and went to live away from the river, near the market, on the edge of the lower town. By the time he got married, he was already living on the even-numbered side of the street (the forbidden side); later, he climbed another rung: he moved to an area where, according to the law, no Jew had the right to be born, to live, to die. He was respected. To his friends and family, he was simultaneously an object of envy and the very symbol of hope: proof that it was indeed possible to attain such heights. Hunger meant nothing; being cold, living in filth meant nothing given such prospects. And from the lowest, poorest part of town, many eyes looked upwards, towards the cool hills where the rich men lived.

Between these two extremes was a middle ground, a drab land where neither great poverty nor great wealth existed, where the Russian, Polish and Jewish middle classes lived together, more or less in peace.

Yet even here, halfway up the hill, the community was divided into little groups who were envious and despised each other. At the top were the doctors, the lawyers, the managers of large estates; at the bottom were the common rabble: shopkeepers, tailors, pharmacists and the like.

But there was one section of society that served as a link between all the different districts, and whose members scraped a living by running from one house to the other, from the lower end of town to the top. Ada's father, Israel Sinner, was one of this brotherhood of *maklers* or go-betweens. Their profession consisted of buying and selling on behalf of other people – beet, sugar, wheat, agricultural machinery, all the usual merchandise of the Ukraine – but they could also get hold of silk and tea, Turkish Delight and coal, caviar from the Volga and fruit from Asia, depending on their clients' needs. They begged, they pleaded, they belittled their rivals' goods; they moaned, they lied, they used every ounce of imagination, all the subtle arts of persuasion to win a commission. You could tell who they were by their rapid speech, their gestures, the way they hurried (at a time and in a country where no one hurried), by their humility, their tenacity, and by the many other qualities unique to them.

Ada, who was still little more than a baby, sometimes went with her father to do his buying. He was a short, thin man with sad eyes who loved her and found comfort simply in holding her hand. For her, he walked more slowly; he bent towards her anxiously, made sure the heavy grey wool shawl she wore over her old coat and little brown velvet hat with ear flaps were properly arranged, cupped his hand over her mouth in winter: on the street corners, the bitter wind seemed to lie in wait for the passers-by and slap their faces with joyful ferocity.

'Be careful. Are you cold?' her father would ask.

And he told her to breathe through her shawl so that the freezing air would warm up a bit as it passed through the wool. But it was impossible: she felt she was suffocating. As soon as he looked away, she used her fingernail to make the little hole in the shawl a bit bigger and tried to catch snowflakes on the end of her tongue. She was so thoroughly wrapped up that all you could see of her was a small square bundle on top of thin legs, and, from close up, two large black eyes peering out between the dark cap and the grey shawl; her eyes looked even bigger because of the dark circles beneath them, and their expression was as intense and fearful as a wild young animal's.

She had just turned five and was beginning to take in everything around her. Until now, she had wandered about in a world so out of proportion to her scrawny body that she barely realised it existed; it dwarfed her. She gave it no more thought than an insect hidden in the grass might. But she was older now and determined to know life: those motionless giants standing in the doorways, icicles hanging from their moustaches, who breathed out the fetid odour of alcohol (curiously, their breath seemed to transform into a spurt of steam, then into little needles of snow), were in fact ordinary men, *dvorniks*, caretakers who looked after the houses. And those other men whose heads seemed to disappear into the clouds and who dragged shining sabres behind them, they were called 'officers'. They were frightening because whenever her father saw them he clung to the walls and seemed to try to make himself even smaller. But, despite this, she believed they belonged to the human race. For a while now, she'd dared look at them: a few of them wore grey greatcoats lined in red (you could see the scarlet fabric, symbol of their rank of General, when they climbed into the sleighs), and some of them had long white beards, like her grandfather.

At the town square, she stopped for a moment to admire the horses. In winter, they wore green or red blankets decorated with pom-poms, so that the snow they kicked up didn't fly on to their backs. The square was the heart of the town – there were beautiful hotels, shops, restaurants, lights and bustle – but soon she and her father descended once more down the narrow, steep streets that sloped towards the river, had gaps in the paving stones, and were poorly lit by lanterns, until finally they stopped in front of the home of some potential client.

In a smoke-filled, half-lit room with a low ceiling, five or six men were screaming, like chickens whose throats were being slit. Their faces were all red; their veins throbbed on their foreheads. They raised their arms and pointed to the heavens or beat their chests.

'May God strike me dead on the spot if I'm lying!' they said.

Sometimes, they pointed to Ada. 'I swear to God on the life of this innocent child that the silk wasn't torn when I bought it! Is it *my* fault, me, a poor Jew with a family to feed, if the mice got at some of it while it was in transit?'

They argued, they walked out, they slammed the doors; on the doorstep, they stopped, they came back. The buyers drank tea from large glasses in silver holders, feigning an air of indifference. The go-betweens (there were always five or six of them who showed up at the same time once they'd caught wind of a deal) accused each other of cheating, theft, fraud or worse; they looked as if they might tear each other to pieces. Then everything calmed down: a deal had been struck.

Ada's father took her hand and they left. Once in the street, he let out a long, deep sigh that ended with a nod of his head and a mournful, heavy moan: 'Oh, my God, my dear God!' Sometimes he groaned because the *gescheft*, the deal, hadn't worked out, and all his efforts, the weeks of endless discussions and schemes had been in vain; sometimes because he'd actually managed to win out over his rivals. But he had to sigh or moan no matter what happened: God was immovable and ever-present, like a spider at the centre of its web, stalking man and ready to punish anyone who seemed proud to be happy. God was always there, fervent and jealous; it was necessary to fear Him and, while simultaneously thanking Him for His goodness, also to make sure that He didn't believe He had granted all of His creature's wishes, so that He didn't lose interest and continued to provide protection.

Afterwards, they visited another house, and then another. Sometimes they even went up to the wealthy homes. Ada would wait in the entrance hall, so overwhelmed by the magnificent furniture, the number of servants and the thickness of the carpets, that she dared not move. She sat dead still on the edge of a chair, staring wide-eyed and trying not to breathe; sometimes she pinched her cheeks so she wouldn't fall asleep. Finally, they would return home on the tram, in silence, holding hands.

2

'Simon Arkadievich,' said Ada's father, 'I'm like the Jew who went to complain to a *zadik*, a holy man, to ask his advice about his poverty . . .'

Israel Sinner mimed the encounter between the poor man and the saint:

'"Oh, Holy One, I am poverty stricken; I have ten children to feed, a difficult wife, a mother-in-law in perfect health, with a hearty appetite and plenty of energy . . . What shall I do? Help me!"

'And the holy man replied: "Get twelve goats and let them live with you."

'"But what will I do with them? We're already piled one on top of the other like herrings in a barrel; we all sleep on thin straw mattresses. We're suffocating. What will I do with your goats?"

'"Hear me, ye of little faith. Take the goats into your house and you will be glorifying God."

'A year later, the poor man returned: "Well, are you happier?"

'"Happy? My life is a living Hell! I'll kill myself if I have to keep those damned animals!"

'"Well, now you can get rid of them and you will appreciate the happiness you didn't realise was yours before. Without their stench and their butting horns, your poor hovel will seem like a palace to you. Everything on this earth is relative."

'In the same way, Simon Arkadievich, I complained about my Fate. I had my father-in-law to lodge and my daughter to feed. It was hard to find work and they had little to eat. But it is natural for man to sweat a great deal to earn a little bread. I was wrong to complain. Now I find that my brother has died and my sister-in-law, his widow, is coming to live with me with her two children. Three more mouths to feed. Work, toil, pitiful man, poor Jew: you can rest when you are deep beneath the ground . . .'

That was how Ada learned of the existence and imminent arrival of her cousins. She tried to picture their faces. It was a game that kept her occupied for hours on end; she saw and heard nothing of what was happening around her, then seemed to wake up as if out of some dream. She heard her father say to Simon Arkadievich:

'Someone told me about a shipment of raisins from Smyrna. Are you interested?'

'Leave me in peace! What would I do with your raisins?'

'Don't get angry, don't get angry . . . I could get you some cotton from Nijni cheap?'

'To hell with your cotton!'

'What would you say to a batch of ladies' hats from Paris, just a tiny bit damaged after a railway accident? They're still being held at the border and would cost half what they're worth.'

'Hmm . . . how much?'

When they were in the street, Ada asked: 'Are my aunt and cousins going to live with us?'

'Yes.'

They were walking down an enormous empty boulevard. As a result of ambitious planning, a number of new avenues intersected the town; they were wide enough for a squadron to march between the double row of lime trees, but only the wind rushed from one end to the other, swirling the dust around with a sharp, joyous whistle. It was a summer's evening, beneath a clear, red sky.

'There'll be a woman in the house,' Ada's father finally said, looking sadly at her, 'someone to take care of you . . .'

'I don't want anyone to take care of me.'

He shook his head. 'Someone to stop the servant from stealing, and I won't have to drag you around with me all day . . .'

'Don't you like me coming with you?' asked Ada, her little voice trembling.

He stroked her hair gently: 'Of course I do, but I have to walk slowly so your legs don't get tired, and we brokers earn our living by running. The faster we run, the quicker we get to the rich people's homes. Other brokers earn more than me because they run faster than me: they can leave their children at home, where it's nice and warm.'

'With their wives . . .' he thought. But you weren't supposed to speak of the dead, out of a superstitious fear of attracting the attention of disease or misfortune (demons were always lying in wait), and so as not to upset the child. She had plenty of time to learn how difficult life was, how uncertain, how it was always poised to steal the things you cherished most . . . And anyway, the past was the past. If you dwelt on it, you lost the strength you needed to keep going. That was why Ada had to grow up barely ever hearing her dead mother's name, or anything about her or her brief life. There was a faded photograph in the house of a young girl in a school uniform with long dark hair spilling down over her shoulders. Half-hidden behind the heavy curtain, the portrait seemed to watch the living with a look of reproach: 'I was also once like you' those eyes seemed to say. 'Why are you afraid of me?' But no matter how shy, how sweet she may have been, she was still frightening, she who lived in a realm where there was no food, no sleep, no fear, no angry arguments, nothing, actually, that resembled the fate of humans on this earth.

Ada's father feared the arrival of his sister-in-law and her children, but really, the house was too neglected, too dirty, and his little girl needed a woman to look after her. As for himself, he was resigned to never being anything but a poor man, uneducated, even though he'd dreamt of better things when he'd got married . . . But his own desires, he himself, in the end, counted for little. You worked, you lived, you had hopes for your children. Weren't they your flesh and blood? If Ada managed to have more than he had on this earth, he'd be happy. He imagined her wearing a beautiful embroidered dress with a bow in her hair, like the rich children. How could he know how to dress a child? She looked old-fashioned and sickly in her clothes; they were too big and too long. He'd bought them because the fabric was of good quality, but sometimes the colours didn't go well together . . . He glanced over at the Tartan dress she was wearing with the little black velvet bodice that Nastasia, the cook, had made. He didn't like his daughter's hairstyle either, that thick fringe on her forehead that came right down to cover her eyebrows, and the uneven dark ringlets around her neck. Her poor little thin neck . . . He put his hand around the back of her neck and gently squeezed it, his heart bursting with tenderness. But since he was Jewish, it wasn't enough to dream of his little girl with plenty to eat, well cared for, and, later on, making a good marriage. He would love to find within her some talent, some extraordinary gift. Perhaps she could one day be a musician or a famous actress? His desires were modest and limited out of necessity, since he only had a daughter. Ah, vain wishes, hopes dashed! A son! A boy! It hadn't been God's will, but he consoled himself with the thought that the sons of his friends, far from being the delight of their twilight years, were the affliction, the disgrace and the obvious punishment inflicted by the Lord: they were involved in politics; they were imprisoned or exiled by the government; others wandered from one place to another, far away, in foreign cities. Not that he would object to sending Ada to study in Switzerland, Germany or France when she was older ... But he had to work, tirelessly save money. He looked at the filthy little notebook where he made notes on the various merchandise he had to sell, and walked faster.

3

In the evenings they drank tea, squeezed together on the leather settee in the narrow dining room, one glass after another of strong, hot tea, with a slice of lemon in it and a sugar lump to nibble, until Ada fell asleep in her seat. The kitchen door was always left open, allowing the smoke from the stove to pour into the room. Nastasia rummaged through the dishes, stirred the wood in the stove, sometimes singing as she went, or muttering, her voice sounding tipsy. Barefoot, wearing a scarf on her head, she was fat, heavy, flabby and smelled of alcohol; she suffered from chronic toothache, and an old faded shawl framed her wide red face. Nevertheless, she was the 'Messalina' of the neighbourhood, and rare were the nights when there wasn't a pair of boots belonging to one of the local soldiers standing in the kitchen, just in front of the dirty, torn curtain that screened off her bed.

Ada's maternal grandfather lived with his son-in-law. He was a handsome elderly man, his face adorned with a white beard; he had a long thin nose and a receding hairline. His life had been strange: when he'd been a very young man, he'd escaped from the ghetto and travelled in Russia and Europe. He hadn't been motivated by a desire for wealth, but rather a thirst for know-ledge. He'd come home as poor as when he'd left, but with a trunk full of books. His father had died and he had to support his mother and find husbands for his sisters. He had never spoken a word to anyone about his travels, his experiences or his dreams. He had taken over his father's jewellery business: he sold moderately priced silver, along with rings and brooches decorated with gemstones from the Urals which newlyweds from the lower town liked to buy. But even though he spent his days behind a counter, when night fell, he padlocked and chained his door closed and opened the trunk of books. He would take out a wad of paper and the old quill pen that made a scratching sound and work on his book, a book that Ada would never see completed; all she would ever know was its incomprehensible title: 'The Character and Defence of Shylock'.

The shop was on the ground floor of the Sinners' house. After evening tea, it was her grandfather's habit to go down into the shop, the manuscript under his arm and carrying a small pot of ink and his pen. An oil lamp burned on the table, while the stove, filled with logs, roared, spreading warmth and casting a reddish glow throughout the room. Ada, whose father had gone back to town, would leave Nastasia in the arms of her soldier, and go downstairs to sit beside her grandfather, rubbing her heavy, tired eyes. She would slide silently on to a chair next to the wall. Her grandfather would read or write. An icy draught slipped through the crack in the door and made the end of his long beard flutter. These winter nights, full of tranquil melancholy, were the sweetest moments of Ada's life. But they were about to be lost because of the arrival of Aunt Raissa and her children.

Aunt Raissa was a thin, energetic, dry woman with a pointy nose and chin, a scathing tongue and eyes as sharp and shining as the point of a needle. She was rather vain about her slim figure, which she made look even slimmer by wearing a narrow buckled belt and the full corset popular at the time. She was a redhead; the contrast between her flamboyant hair and her thin, aging body was strange and painful to behold. She wore her hair like the French cabaret singer Yvette Guilbert, with thousands of tiny red curls falling on to her forehead and temples. She stood up very straight, her small bosom thrust slightly back in her effort to stand tall. She had thin, tight lips, darting eyes beneath half-closed lids, and a piercing, frightening expression that missed nothing. When she was in a good mood, she had a peculiar way of puffing herself up and slightly moving her shoulders that made her look like a long, thin insect flapping its wings. Because of her slimness, her vivacity and jaunty maliciousness, she resembled a wasp.

In the days of her youth, Aunt Raissa had had many admirers – at least, that was what she implied with her little sighs. She was an ambitious creature; her husband had been the owner of a printing works, and she felt that her widowhood had forced her down into a lower social class. *She*, who had met intellectuals, she would say with a proud little scornful smile hovering about her lips, she was now no more than a poor relation! She'd been taken in out of charity. She had to live, supreme indignity, in the Jewish quarter, above a miserable shop.

'But really, Isa,' she would say to her brother-in-law, 'don't you owe it to your good name to raise your children somewhere cleaner, with a better reputation? *You* seem to have forgotten, but as long as I live, I will never forget that my poor husband's name, and yours as well, is Sinner.'

Ada listened to her, sitting in her usual place, on the old settee, between her cousins, Lilla and Ben. It must have been shortly after Aunt Raissa's arrival. It was one of Ada's earliest memories. They were drinking their evening tea. Her grandfather, her father and Aunt Raissa were sitting on cane chairs with dark wooden backs that were called, she never knew why, 'Viennese chairs', even though they'd been bought second-hand from the man on the square, while the children sat on the brown leather settee with its tall, stiff back. To Ada, the house had always seemed dark and unwelcoming, which it was, to tell the truth . . . It was an old building; its four rooms led off to small, dimly-lit corridors with large cupboards, and the rooms were all on different levels so that in order to walk around the entire house, you had to go up and down rickety staircases, and through icy spaces paved with brick and serving no particular purpose. When night fell they were lit by the pale, flickering light of a street lamp out in the courtyard. Ada often felt afraid in this house, but the settee was a haven to her: she loved it there. It was where she waited for her father, where she fell asleep at night while everyone around her talked, not thinking to send her to bed. Behind the cushions, she hid old pictures, broken toys – the ones she loved most – and coloured pencils. The settee was worn out; the torn leather hung down in ribbons in places, the springs creaked. But she loved it. Now it was Ben's bed; she felt ejected, cast out.

She held her cup of tea in both hands and blew on it with such concentration that her little face seemed to disappear into the large cup and all you could see of her was her thick, dark-brown fringe.

Her aunt looked at her and, wishing to be kind, said: 'Come here, Adotchka. I'll tie back your hair with a pretty ribbon, darling.'

Ada obediently stood up, but she had to make her way through the narrow space left between people's legs and the table, and it took her a long time. When she finally arrived, her aunt had forgotten all about her. Ada slipped on to her father's lap and listened to the grown-ups talk, while trying to poke her finger through the smoke rings that came from her father's cigarette; it made little bluish rings, light and moist, that disappeared as soon as she reached out to touch them.

'We are the Sinner family,' Aunt Raissa said with pride. 'And who is the richest man in this town? Old Salomon Sinner. And in Europe?'

She turned towards Ada's grandfather. 'You've travelled, Ezekiel Lvovich, have you ever seen the family's mansions in London and Vienna?'

'We're not as closely related as that,' Ada's father said, laughing slightly in surprise.

'Really? Not closely related? And just what makes you say that, if you please? Wasn't your own grandmother the first cousin of old Sinner? Both of them ran barefoot through the mud. Then she married your grandfather who sold clothes and old furniture, in Berdichev.'

'They're called rag merchants,' Ben said suddenly.

'Keep your mouth shut,' his mother said harshly, 'you don't know what you're talking about! Rag merchants carry bundles of old clothes on their backs and go door to door trying to sell them in the slums. Your grandfather had a shop and an assistant, two assistants, when things were going well. Back then, Salomon Sinner worked hard, made money, and his sons did well and made even more money, so much so that today their fortune is worth at least as much as the Rothschilds'.'

But now, given the incredulous looks on their faces, she could sense she had gone too far.

'They may have a few million less than the Rothschilds, two or three million less, I can't remember, but they are hugely wealthy and we're related to them. That's what we mustn't forget. If you were to put yourself forward a bit more, my poor Isa, and stop looking like a sad little dog – you've looked like that since the day you were born – as your brother always said, you could be someone in this town. Money is money, but blood is blood.'

'Money . . .' her father said quietly.

He sighed, smiled slightly. Everyone fell silent. He poured a little tea into his saucer and drank it, nodding his head. Everyone thought money a good thing, but to a Jew, it was a necessity, like air or water. How could they live without money? How could they pay the bribes? How could they get their children into school when there were already too many students enrolled? How could they buy permission to go here or there, to sell this or that? How could they avoid military service? Oh, my God! Without money, how could they live?

Her grandfather moved his lips slightly and tried to recall the quotation from a Psalm he needed for chapter XII, paragraph 7 of his book. His family's chatter simply did not exist as far as he was concerned. The external world was only important to base creatures who didn't know how to shut it out through spiritual meditation and intellectual thought.

Aunt Raissa looked at the shabby, messy room, full of smoke from the kitchen, and could barely hide her disgust. The wallpaper, a dingy green decorated with silver leaves, was dirty and torn. The only plush armchair was threadbare and wobbly. From the riverbank they could hear the unearthly shouting of a drunkard being beaten by police. She had given up all hope of increasing her fortune by herself now. She'd done her very best in the past, though. When she was single, she hadn't been content to allow a marriage broker to find her a husband; she'd looked for a suitable man herself amongst the university students in the town because they were responsible and intelligent, they had good prospects. Several times, she had gone on the prowl, tirelessly . . . until finally one of them fell into the trap – and how much trouble she had gone to! How many silk skirts had she patiently hemmed, how many old hats mended in her room, in the silence of the night. How many long walks had she taken along the wide avenues of her hometown where, at dusk, young men and unmarried women paraded themselves. She'd had to endure lascivious glances, crude comments. And all her craftiness, the endless, unrelenting schemes to finally steal the chosen one from her more beautiful or richer friends! It had been such a long, cruel, silent war. But what could she do now, a helpless, penniless widow?

She was old, and the husband she had conquered after so many battles – a good husband, owner of the town's first printing works – had died suddenly, leaving her to bring up two children, the pretty Lilla, aged twelve, and that rascal Ben! Lilla was her only hope.

Lilla and Ben were sitting up very straight, next to each other. Lilla was a brunette with pale skin, an innocent, serious, pretty face, a schoolgirl's dress and hair tied back with a black satin ribbon at the base of her neck. Ben had long black curls and a thin, translucent neck. They glanced around the room with curious, frightened faces, though Ben himself seemed less afraid than mocking. He was six years old and small for his age, but his expression was sarcastic, shrewd and bitter, if such emotions are possible in someone so young, and they made him appear older. Sometimes he had the look of a sly, sickly monkey. His face was never at rest; his features constantly quivered; he spoke little, but his eyes, his smile, were eloquent. His hands trembled, his lips moved; he copied the gestures of his mother, his uncle, his grandfather, not simply to mock them, but out of some unconscious imitation. He was passionate about everything: he lifted the lid of the sugar bowl to study a fly that had got trapped inside; he screwed up his eyes, made a horrible face, leaned forward to better see how its little feet moved, caught it in his hand, threw it into Ada's cup. He got hold of his uncle's watch and opened it with his agile fingers, made the needles go round. Every so often, he'd slip away, go over to the window and press his pale, angular little face to the panes of glass, but they were covered in ice. He turned his head this way and that, with quick little movements; his breath etched out a dingy, moist circle in the frosty patterns, so he could see the street where the lights were out in all the shops, where not a single soul passed by. Then he'd go back and sit down again next to Lilla.

On the old, smoke-tinged ceiling, amidst the stains and shadows,

Ada looked for a thin white face, a face only she could see by tilting her head at a certain angle; the face leaned down towards her and gestured to her, mysteriously. Ada smiled, snuggled up in her father's arms, closed her eyes and fell asleep.

4

Ada was seven years old and had more or less grown accustomed to living with her aunt and cousins. Lilla and Ben didn't bother her. Her aunt only paid attention to her in the presence of her father, who no longer took her with him to work, now that he needn't worry about her. And so she was even more alone than before; she played silently on the old settee or in the courtyard. On Sundays, Lilla took her out. It was convenient for Lilla to have her little cousin with her when she met with boys from the local schools; she could count on Ada to run ahead obediently, to remain silent, when they got home, about what had actually happened, and to confirm all her lies.

In winter, the young people met up in the tea shops (they were of an age when love stimulates the appetite); they consumed an alarming number of heart-shaped pastries filled with cream and sprinkled with pink sugar, some of which they generously offered to Ada. They had to be careful as they ate not to let any crumbs fall into the folds of their coats as a tell-tale sign to the shrewd eyes of their mothers.

When talking about Lilla, her mother always said, with a sarcastic little snigger: 'My daughter could never fool me. A robber never gets robbed.' This local saying meant that no one could be cleverer than someone who had spent his whole life playing the worst tricks on others to benefit himself. And Aunt Raissa certainly seemed to know what she was talking about . . . Yet she never noticed Lilla's flushed cheeks, the rings under her eyes, her dishevelled hair when she came home. In summer, the young people would meet at one of the four public gardens: Nicolas Square, the Botanical Gardens, the Tsar's Garden and Merchant's Place. On hazy Sundays, they would walk arm in arm around the band stand, the girls in straw hats, the tops of their dresses stretched taut over their blossoming breasts, their skirts billowing around their hips, and the boys in light shirts, their belts with the Imperial Eagle around their waists and their caps tipped backwards, looking as if they could conquer the world. They exchanged longing glances and love letters. The brass instruments of the military band resounded through the pink evening. Supervisors from their schools wandered about, spying on the courting couples; the rules were strict. But there were ways around them: they met far away from the gates, at nightfall. They strolled slowly down empty streets where the only person in sight was the man ringing his bell to sell ice cream. Ada's cousin gave her a little cup of chocolate ice cream and she ran on ahead of the couple, watching out for any suspicious figures in the houses, whistling if she saw a passer-by, while the ice cream slowly melted in the warm evening air.

One spring day, Lilla and her admirer had gone for a walk in the Botanical Gardens, Ada following behind. It was a rather isolated, overgrown spot. Some sleepy animals lived in iron cages: an eagle from the Caucasus crawling with vermin, some wolves, a bear panting with thirst. One of the cages was empty; its previous inhabitants, some foxes, had dug a hole in the ground and escaped a few years before, or so the story went. All that remained were the iron bars, a large, rusty lock, and a sign swaying in the wind that read: 'Foxes'. But Ada always hoped that one of the young cubs might have come back home. She pressed her face against the bars and called out, 'Come on, let's see you, I won't tell anyone you're here.' But in vain. Finally, disappointed, she would walk away, throwing a crust of bread to the eagle and the wolves. Ill and indifferent, the animals never stirred. She glanced furtively over at Lilla, seated next to that day's lucky boy, a nice fifteen-year-old secondary school student. Lilla had forgotten her. Ada was bored; the mosquitoes were eating up her bare arms. She walked slowly along the paths, then hopped until she got to two blocks of stone that the locals called 'didko' and 'babko', the grandfather and the grandmother; their worn-out features vaguely resembled human faces. Ada had been told they were pagan idols from the past: the god of storms and his wife, the queen of fertility. At their feet, it was still possible to see the plinth where sacrifices were made, and a drain carved into the stone where the victims' blood would run. But to Ada, they were familiar friends – they really were a grandmother and grandfather dozing outside their house, warmed by the sun. She had built a little hut of dead leaves and branches behind them, no higher than a molehill, and she imagined it was their house, that they'd come outside to rest in the sunshine and that they would go back inside when it got dark. She made a crown of yellow daisies and placed it on the head of the savage idol; the daisies had dark centres and a bitter smell. Then she climbed up on to the shoulders of the old god of storms and stroked him, as if he were a dog, but she soon got bored.

She went and tugged on Lilla's skirt. 'Come on,' she said, 'let's go for a walk.'

Lilla sighed. She was too gentle and soft to oppose Ada for long. She wished she could bribe her with sweets or those red balloons called 'mother-in-laws' tongues' which made a shrill noise when you let the air out. But Ada wasn't to be bought off with promises, and neither Lilla nor her boyfriend had any money left.

They left their mossy, leafy hiding place in the Botanical Gardens and headed up towards the top of the hill.

The houses were so beautiful! Ada had never been there before. She went up to each of the high, closed gates and looked at the large gardens planted with lime trees. Every now and again, a horse and carriage passed by. Everything here radiated wealth and calm. In front of one of the gilded gates, Ada saw a carriage stop. A young boy the same age as Ben came out of the house, accompanied by a woman. Ada had never before seen anyone dressed like that. All the boys she knew wore school uniforms, or shabby clothes if they lived in the Jewish quarter. This boy wore a suit of light beige silk and a large fine linen collar, but his resemblance to Ben was so striking: he had the same black curls, fine nose, long, delicate neck – too long: it tilted forward and made him look like a curious bird – and the same wide eyes, simultaneously bright and misty, like a light burning in oil . . . She grabbed Lilla's hand and, at a loss for words, nodded towards the boy. The carriage pulled away.

'They're the Sinners,' said Lilla's friend. Then he looked at her and said, 'They have the same last name as you, don't they? Are you related?'

'I don't know. I don't think so,' murmured Lilla, blushing at the thought of the difference between this house and hers in the lower town.

'They're rich Jews,' the boy said, sounding both respectful and mocking, a strange and subtle mixture of emotions that even Ada, small as she was, could identify. 'The kid's name is Harry.'

He put his arm around Lilla's waist.

'Cover your eyes and count to a hundred,' he ordered Ada.

Ada obeyed. Lilla and the boy kissed for a long time. Ada watched them through her fingers. Then she got bored; she climbed on to a stone and looked through the gate at the spacious, aristocratic house with its columns and shady lime trees.

Until this moment she'd been happy simply to take in what was going on around her with the natural curiosity of an intelligent child. Looking at the outside world had never brought her any particular pleasure. Now, however, she suddenly felt it. Sweet and deep, it pierced her like an arrow. For the first time, she truly saw the lovely colour of the sky, lilac and pistachio green, like sorbet; a yellowish moon, pale and round, without a halo, hovered there in the daylight. And on the horizon she could see soft, fluffy little clouds rushing by; they looked as if the moon was breathing them in, absorbing them. Ada had never seen anything quite as beautiful as that sky. Ada had never seen anything quite as beautiful as the Sinners' house. Evening was falling. She looked up at the windows where the lights were being lit, and tried to guess which one was Harry's room. She decided it was the one on the right that shone as brightly as a star. She pressed her cheek against the iron bars of the gate.

'Harry . . . Harry . . . Harry . . .' she whispered.

She felt the same exquisite yet somewhat painful pleasure she'd felt when she looked at the beautiful house and the sky. She spoke this strange, mysterious name, with its unique and noble sound, as if it were a kiss.

5

Nastasia washed the windows once a year, just before Passover. The rest of the time, they remained grubby, soiled by the rain on the outside and by children's breath and dirty hands on the inside. Even on the most beautiful days, the rooms were half in darkness. Ada, however, never noticed this until the year she and Ben were ill at the same time and had to stay in bed for nearly a month in Ada's room.

It was an attic room with a yellow-painted floor and wallpaper decorated with Chinese figures. During their fever, Ada and Ben passed the hours by quietly counting to themselves the number of people they could see from their bed. The Chinamen wore large straw hats and had bare legs; leaning on their canes, they watched coy Chinese women with parasols. Some of the parasols were red and some blue, but because of a nearby drainpipe, dark stains of damp had blurred the colours, merging them into a shade of purple that faded from plum to the colour of amaranth. Just above each bed, the children's frustrated little fingers had torn away the paper and they'd used crayons to draw faces and animals on the bare plaster. In a corner of the room, a spider's web hung from the ceiling and, before the Passover spring clean, it swayed in the draft that endlessly wafted in from the kitchen. The door at the back of the flat was always left open so that Nastasia's lovers could come up whenever they wanted.

Whenever Ada and Ben were ill, Aunt Raissa would heat a little pork fat mixed with turpentine over the flame of a candle and, with her thin, dry hands, rub it over the children's backs and chests. Then she would make them drink gallons of boiling hot tea, and when the symptoms seemed really serious, she would place a hot compress to their necks and make them swallow a spoonful of castor oil. To ease the terrible taste of the medicine, Lilla secretly brought them little buns filled with hard-boiled egg which she bought in town, along with sticky sweets that had spent over a week in the pockets of her admirers. And so Ben and Ada usually welcomed illness. But this time it was really lasting too long. Their fever, sluggishness, sore throats and painful ears seemed interminable. After all, they couldn't sleep all the time, nor cut out endless puppets from bits of paper: it was too boring. Finally, towards the end of the third week, Ben had a brilliant idea, which transformed their gloomy days.

They had begun by playing the game of 'islands', dividing imaginary lands between them, as all children do; but that wasn't enough. Later on, they couldn't remember which of them had been the first to invent what they called 'the game', the one that replaced all others. This is how it went: under the supervision of Ada and Ben, all children had to meet one morning and leave in search of a foreign land (one they would of course find), and there they would live entirely alone, without a single adult ever being allowed in. They would have their own laws, their own army, their own government. The masons' children would build the cities; the painters' children would certainly know how to decorate the walls. The place had to be inaccessible, protected by high rocks, even though no one would ever dream of coming to look for them; the grown-ups would be only too happy, or so they thought, to be rid of all the children! Well, didn't they hear their parents moaning endlessly? Everything was so expensive! Clothing, food, education . . . And when they were older, they had to provide dowries for the girls, help the boys set up in business. There was so much to worry about . . . Surely they would be delighted to know they were alive and well, far away.

Eyes closed, her cheeks flushed with fever, Ada imagined them leaving. It was daybreak. Or, even better, pitch dark, in the middle of the night, while everyone was asleep. From every house, the children emerged, barefoot so as not to make any noise, and each carrying a lantern (that was the most important thing), hidden under their coats to dim the light. They gathered together somewhere beyond the village, and set off. They walked more quickly than their old, heavy parents, of course. Even if they wanted to catch up to them, it would be impossible. Ada could picture every one of them: children from her neighbourhood, from the town, from all over Russia, slender, supple shadows, huddled together, bedding down in a dark forest or beside the riverbanks. They would walk for a long time, for weeks, months if necessary, before finally arriving in the land that awaited them, wherever that might be, but she felt as if she could see it. There were wild animals so they could enjoy hunting, and enemies for when they played at war, and dry earth so they could have the satisfaction of working and building something.

'What should we call it, Ben?'

But they could never agree on a name.

'What if they send the police to find us?'

'Why should they? Do you think anyone would miss us?'

'Well, you remember when that little Rose, the tailor's daughter, died last year, how her mother cried . . .'

'But she was dead, you silly; we'll be very much alive, we will!'

'But what if they get angry because we ran off without their permission and send the police to bring us back?'

Ben's eyes sparkled. 'The Emperor's children will be with us. The police will surely obey them!'

'You think that the Emperor's children will come with us?'

'Of course. They're children just like us. Don't you think they'd like to be free, to build houses, and buy and sell things in shops?'

Day after day, the game became more embellished with details and new adventures. The children would have uniforms, medals, books they'd written, streets, laws.

'But who would be in charge?'

They glanced furtively at each other: the little boy lying on his back, his sheet and the grey woollen shawl he used as a blanket pulled up to his chin; the little girl sitting up against her pillow, leaning on one elbow. All she could see of Ben was the tip of his quivering nose, long and thin, half hidden by his dark curls. Impatiently, she tugged on her brown fringe; her lips were dry from the fever, her cheeks scarlet. She wore a short day dress and one of Lilla's old cardigans. The sleeves were too long and you could see her bare, thin arms twitching. She didn't own any night-dresses; it seemed perfectly natural to spend money on clothing people would see, but not on things they wouldn't. She gestured quickly, decisively.

'Neither of us would be in charge, because we could only ever be equals. If we were in charge, we'd have two governments and we'd be at war.'

'Well, why couldn't we both be in charge?' asked Ben. 'You could command the girls and me the boys.'

'But we'd have to have one supreme leader to decide who was the winner, you fool!'

'Once we'd well and truly beaten you, we wouldn't need anyone to decide who the winner was!'

'But while the war was going on,' cried Ada, totally overexcited, 'while we were fighting, who would be in charge? To look after . . .'

She made a vague gesture. 'The others . . . the ones who didn't want to fight . . .'

'Well, who do you suggest?' said Ben, defiantly.

Ada lowered her eyes and said softly: 'Harry Sinner.'

Just speaking his name made her heart ache. She'd kept her secret for a long time: six months had passed since the moment she had first laid eyes on him, and she hadn't seen him again. But she had never forgotten him, and to say his name out loud made him suddenly appear, between Ben and her, in their shabby room.

Ben sniggered: 'Why him?'

'Why? He's bigger than you,' she shouted, her voice quivering indignantly. With that knowing feminine instinct that can aim straight at the vulnerable place in a man's heart, she had sought, and found, the worst insult. (Ben was small for an eight-year-old boy.)

'He's at least that much taller than you,' she said, lifting her hand up to Harry's height, 'and he's stronger too! He knows things you don't. He knows how to ride.'

'Have you seen him riding?'

She didn't want to say anything untrue, so she just nodded.

'You're lying!'

'No I'm not!'

For a few seconds they shouted 'are too' and 'am not' at each other, their faces contorted in anger. They screamed at the top of their voices. When they stopped, hoarse and exhausted by the violence of their shouting, they could hear Nastasia singing wistfully in the kitchen. Aunt Raissa had gone to buy a few things from Alchwang, the tailor who dressed the city's middle classes; the men were out at work and Lilla was at school.

'Swear then!' Ben said finally.

Ada swore like Nastasia did: she quickly crossed herself.

'I swear on the Holy Cross!'

'It's not hard to ride a horse,' said Ben after a moment's silence.

'What's hard is to buy a horse. But he wouldn't know how to climb up the back of a tram, hang on and get around town like that, without being seen by the police, or how to lead a gang of kids from the Jewish quarter against a gang from the marketplace, or how to fight one against ten . . .'

'And you fought one against ten? When?'

'More times than you've had hot dinners,' Ben replied, deeply resentful, imitating the biting reply Nastasia had made to her rival, the woman who sold herrings, who'd accused her of never having had a marriage proposal from any of her lovers.

But they were tired of shouting and getting upset, so Ada and Ben fell silent. Night was already falling: it was the early dusk of winter. A cockroach slowly crossed the room, twitching its feelers; others climbed up the wall, attracted by the warmth from the wood-burning stove. They were never chased away: they were a sign of wealth in a house. Through the frozen windowpane, they could just make out the shoemaker's sign next door: a boot made of golden metal, decorated with spurs, all covered in snow and lit up by the low flame of a gaslight in the street. Everything was still, but it was an empty, joyless stillness. Ada buried her cheeks and forehead in the pillow and closed her eyes. Beneath her lowered eyelids, she pictured a long road in the dead of night, but it was a summer's night, warm and dark. She was walking with Harry. Harry was tired and he was leaning against her; Harry was hungry and she gave him food. Then she was the one who was afraid, who was cold, who was in pain, and Harry consoled her, reassured her, took care of her. The game transformed into a dream: the images were detailed, but bathed in a peculiar light, pale and grey, like the first breaking of dawn, and the sounds (the voices of the children who were running away with them, Harry's laughter, their footsteps along the road), all the sounds were clear, yet somehow muffled, distant. Harry! What a wonderful name . . . The name of a true prince . . . That name alone would have been enough to make her fall in love, even if she had never seen his face or his house . . . To be allowed inside, even just to cross the threshold, to see Harry's room, his toys . . . He might let her touch them. He might even take books, coloured crayons, balls and pile them into Ada's arms, saying, 'Here. We can share.'

She thought she could almost hear him whispering in her ear. She sank deeper into a feverish sleep. She could feel her imaginary friend's cheek next to hers, a cheek as cool and soft as a piece of fruit. She took his hand and fell asleep.

6

The Jews who lived in the lower town were religious and fanatically attached to their customs; the Jews in the wealthy areas were strict observers of tradition. To the poor Jews, their religion was so completely engrained in them that it would have been just as impossible to extricate themselves from it as to live without their beating hearts. To the rich Jews, loyalty to the rites of their forefathers seemed in good taste, dignified, morally honourable, as much as – perhaps more than – true belief. Between these two classes, each observant in their own fashion, the lower middle classes lived in yet another way. They called upon God to bless their business dealings, heal a relative, a spouse, a child, then forgot about Him straight away, or, if they did think about Him, it was with a mixture of superstitious fear and contained resentment: God never fully granted anything that was asked of Him.

Ada's father went to Synagogue from time to time, in the same way someone might go and see an investor who could help you in business – that is, if he wanted to. He even had the power to drag you once and for all out of the poverty trap, except he had too many protégés, too many people asking favours, and was actually too rich, too great, too powerful to spare a thought for you, a humble earthly creature. But you could always turn up where you knew He would be ... Why not? Perhaps He might notice you? Or when things were going badly, you could remind Him of your existence with a whisper, a sigh: 'Ah! *Bozhe, Bozhenka!* (Ah, my God, my dear sweet God!)', with just a glimmer of hope, with a sad, resigned reproach: why have You abandoned me?

But religious laws were really too complicated, too strict to be followed faithfully; you took your pick: some were observed and some weren't. People fasted one day a year, and during Passover they ate unleavened bread – but with ordinary Russian bread on the same plate, which was a great sin. But they had done it once, by accident, and nothing had happened. God had not cast His wrath upon the family. Life had gone on. When she was very young, Ada had only ever seen adults in her family respect Yom Kippur, the day of fasting (and even that was forgotten later on). Her father had explained to her that it was a very serious day, fearful in the life of man, because God held in His hands a great book, 'like the big accounting book your grandfather has for the shop', and He wrote on one side your good deeds and on the other side your sins. Ada had understood that you had to fast to touch God, but *she* didn't have to fast because she was too young and too thin and anyway, children didn't have that many sins on their conscience. They would acquire them later. She never actually knew whether her father's religious beliefs ended there or if he simply kept the rest to himself since she was too young to really understand.

As for Aunt Raissa, her marriage had taken her into a social class that had evolved even further, one that was proud to distance itself as much as possible from the people they called (and with such scorn!) the simple Jews, the poor Jews.

And so it was that in the Sinner family, Judaism no longer brought any joy, but continued to bring many problems. How they would have liked to leave their fellow Jews to rot in their filth, their poverty and their superstitions. Unfortunately, they couldn't completely forget them because of their horrible lodgings, the ground-floor shop, the street that wasn't exactly the ghetto but was close enough to smell it and hear its screams, not to mention the other, more serious and sometimes tragic inconvenience: the pogroms.

At eight, Ada had never experienced a pogrom, but just as everyone knows about death, she knew there were two dangers – dangers that didn't threaten the rest of humanity, but were directed specifically towards the people of her town, her neighbourhood. Everything could come crashing down on her at any moment, but she might also be spared: this margin of error was enough to reassure her. And the grown-ups she knew talked about this so often that their words no longer had much effect on her, just as a child born near a volcano never thinks about a possible eruption until the day he sees it happen with his very own eyes. The two dangers were pogroms and cholera.

They talked about them in the same way, Ada thought: voices lowered, slowly shaking their heads while sighing and raising their eyes towards heaven. When it was extremely hot and even more people died than usual in the lower town, where the mortality rate was already high; or in springtime, when pilgrims appeared with their vermin and diseases, or when there was a famine, or a drought, everyone would murmur: 'We're in for it this summer...' And whenever any sort of political event happened in Russia, whether good or bad (peace, war, a victory, a defeat, the birth of a long-awaited Imperial heir, an assassination, a trial, revolutionary uprisings or a great need of money), the same anxious voices would whisper: 'We're in for it this year, or next month, or tomorrow, or this very night...'

Ada listened to them with so little attention that when the pogrom finally happened, she didn't realise it; for over a week, they'd been talking about unrest, massacres, shops pillaged, women killed, young girls being... At this they bowed their heads, and

Lilla put an extraordinarily innocent look on her face: 'What are you talking about?' it seemed to say. 'I'm not listening to you, and besides, even if I was, I wouldn't know what you meant.' Lilla was getting prettier every day. She had started to wear her long curls in a chignon, low at the back of her neck; her hair softly billowed out over her temples and small forehead. The contrast between her pale skin and dark hair with its bluish sheen was eye-catching. Her hands were slender and delicate. Despite her secret rendezvous in the town's various parks, despite the few kisses she'd bestowed, she was still a good girl, thought Aunt Raissa, who was experienced enough to know.

Aunt Raissa placed all her hopes in Lilla . . . Lilla was so sweet, so feminine, with her pale skin, her elegant walk and her innate desire to be loved, which made each of her soft, shy gestures graceful and appealing. Charming Lilla . . . Everyone loved her. 'She's a silly goose,' Ben would say, 'but a pretty little goose, sweet and innocent . . .' Then he'd add, 'a goose you'd happily eat up.' At nine, Ben knew more about life than his sister, who was fifteen. Lilla inspired a kind of respect in her mother, mixed with anxiety, in the same way that the owner of a stable of race-horses feels kindness tinged with anxiety towards a pretty young filly who hasn't yet shown what she's capable of; one day she would doubtlessly fulfil the hopes placed in her – if she didn't break her leg at the first hurdle, that is.

Aunt Raissa indulged in the most extravagant dreams when it came to her daughter. It wasn't enough merely to think she'd find a good husband. No! Such things were good enough for other girls, but Lilla . . . a different destiny awaited Lilla. She would be an actress or a dancer . . . Or a great singer at the Opera House. She was so docile, so malleable. Her mother could shape her as she wished. It wasn't as if Ada was going to fulfil any expectations. What a child! Taciturn and insolent by turns, rebellious, her head always in the clouds . . . No, she couldn't worry about Ada. She had enough to think about with her own children. As one of her favourite Russian sayings went: 'The shirt you own is closer to your body than your neighbour's suit.' But when Aunt Raissa said, 'The children . . . my children . . .', she was really thinking only of Lilla. And so when the trouble started, Lilla was sent to stay with the family of one of her classmates. They were Russian Orthodox, so their home was safe. As for Ada and Ben, they would have to see.

That year, Ada discovered her grandfather's books for the first time. She hadn't yet started high school as she'd been ill when the admission tests were held, but a first-year student gave her lessons in exchange for lunch and two pairs of shoes per year. She was a good student; she even displayed a quick, insightful mind, less critical or assertive than Ben's, but which nonetheless annoyed Aunt Raissa.

'Why,' she would ask bitterly, 'are Jewish children either too dim or too intelligent? Lilla thinks like an eight-year-old and Ben replies to the slightest observation like an old man. And now Ada's copying him. Why can't they just be like everyone else, not smarter and not more stupid?'

But no one had an answer to that.

Her grandfather's books were works in Russian and translations of English, German and French classics. An entire universe, hitherto unknown, opened before Ada, a world whose colours were so dazzling that reality paled in comparison and faded away. Boris Godunov, Satan, Athalia, King Lear: they all spoke words charged with meaning; every syllable was inexpressively precious. How could the inane, monotonous words her relatives spoke be of any interest whatsoever, those bits of information Ada found so insignificant as they spread from one person to another: 'I heard that the Governor General has received death threats . . . They're saying that the Chief of Police has been wounded . . . I heard some Jews were arrested . . . What if it's true . . . how awful . . . But even if it isn't true . . . God will protect us . . .'

One evening, just as Ada had put down her book and was about to go to bed, she heard strange, muffled noises coming from the streets below, usually so calm at this time of year. It was February, a time of year that was not very cold but when there was heavy snow and strong winds. What could anyone be doing outside? She walked over to the window, blew on it to melt the ice and saw a crowd of people rushing about the street; every now and again they shouted and blew whistles. Ada stood there, watching, not understanding what was happening, when suddenly Aunt Raissa rushed into the room. Red blotches covered her face, as always when she was angry or in the grip of some violent emotion. She grabbed Ada by the arm and yanked her away from the window.

'What are you doing? You horrible child!' she shouted. (She was clearly happy to have her niece there, so she could take out all her fear and anger on her.) 'You're never around when you're needed, but you manage to get in the way at the worst possible time! . . . You have to be careful, my darling,' she said, her voice changing completely as Ada's father came into the room.

Ada wasn't surprised at this sudden change in tone; she'd already learned that her aunt had two voices and two faces and could glide from abuse to sweetness with unbelievable ease and rapidity. She was doing it now: the anger that hissed from her lips had become as soft and plaintive as the sound of a flute.

'Be sensible, my dear. Shouldn't you have gone to bed ages ago? It's ten o'clock. Come on, Adotchka, go to bed, my darling, but . . .'

She and her brother-in-law glanced furtively at each other.

'Only take off your dress and your shoes.'

'Why?'

The adults said nothing.

'Nothing will happen tonight,' her grandfather said as he too came into the room. 'They'll break a few windows and go home to bed. But when the soldiers come, then . . .'

He said no more. All three of them went cautiously over to the window. The room was lit only by a lamp in the adjoining room, but Ada's father took it and lowered the wick until it was so low that it only gave off a dim, almost imperceptible light, reddish and smoky. Ada looked at them, puzzled. They huddled together in the shadows, whispering, taking turns blowing against the dark glass. But she was at an age when the need to sleep overcomes the body with a sudden, imperative force, like drunkenness. She yawned loudly several times, made her way upstairs to bed in the darkness. She took off only her dress and shoes, as they'd told her to. She slipped in between the sheets, smiling – it was lovely and warm in her old bed – and she fell asleep to the sound of the first stones breaking windows down in the lower town.

7

For a few days the damage was limited to shouting, curses, broken windows as night began to fall. Then everything would calm down. The days were quiet. Nevertheless, the children were no longer allowed to go out, and they spent hours sitting side by side on the old settee, playing the game they'd invented, but which became more embellished, a veritable epic with a cast of thousands, with wars, defeats, sieges, victories. Every evening, new stories emerged from their original invention, like branches sprouting from the trunk of an old tree. Their game left them breathless, excited, mouths dry, dark circles beneath their eyes. As soon as dusk fell, they had nothing else to do, for they were forbidden to light the lamps. No one in the lower town dared breathe, crouched behind closed windows and shutters, in narrow rooms that were dark and hot.

But the day finally came when the real world proved more powerful than their dreams. Ben and Ada had attained such a state of hallucination that neither of them was even listening to what the other was saying. They were both talking at the same time in quiet, steady voices, banging their feet against the wood of the settee, when suddenly the murmuring they had stopped listening to was replaced by a savage, unearthly clamour, so close by that they thought it was coming from their own house, from their walls and old floors. At that moment, the door flew open and someone – they didn't recognise who it was because the face was so disfigured with fear – someone rushed in, grabbed them, pushed them and dragged them out. Ben had lost a shoe and was shouting that he wanted to go back and get it, but no one was listening to him. They were taken through the building, out through the kitchen door and thrown, pushed, pulled by their wrists, their hands, their legs, and finally hoisted up a ladder to an attic.

They fell on to the floor, felt the corner of a trunk and an old candelabra, as they fumbled in the darkness. They were in a junk room in the eaves. Ada's father – they could now recognise his rasping, rapid breathing behind the door – sounded as if his heart was about to burst under the strain of his mad rush and terror.

'Don't move. Don't cry. Hide,' he whispered through the keyhole.

Then he added, even more quietly: 'Don't be afraid . . .'

'But I don't want to stay here!' cried Ada.

'Be quiet, my poor darling! Don't move. Don't say a word. Keep still.'

'But, Papa, we're not going to sleep here!'

'But we're hungry, Uncle!'

They beat the locked door with all the strength their little fists could muster. But her father had hurried back down the ladder and they could hear him pulling it away. As soon as they were alone, Ben calmed down.

'There's no point in shouting. It's no use. He's gone.'

The attic looked out over an indoor courtyard, high and narrow, a deep pit between two large walls. Every now and again, the terrifying noise quietened down; the crowd moved off, and they thought they could hear the sea, risen as if by some miracle into the old street, beating its waves against the house. Sometimes soldiers, tramps, professional looters, hysterical Jews would meet at the entrance to the ghetto, and whatever happened then – Ben and Ada had absolutely no idea what it might be – took place inside the doorways of their own house, on their own doorstep. Then the crowds roared like wild animals. They seemed to hurl themselves like rams against the walls, hitting them, backing off, furiously battering them again to try to knock them down, striking them again and again, in vain.

The children sat on top of the trunk, huddled close together, too stunned even to cry. Little by little, they could make out one or two sounds that rose from the steady din of a thousand voices. Listening attentively, their hands shaking, they eagerly picked out the sounds that frightened them less than the others, because they could recognise them.

'Hear that? That's a window being broken. Can you hear the glass shattering? That's stones being thrown against the walls and the iron shutters of the shop. That's everyone laughing. And there's a woman screaming as if her insides are being ripped out. What's going on? . . . And that, that's soldiers singing. And that . . .'

They fell silent, trying to understand the deep, rhythmic wave of sound rising towards them.

'That's prayers,' said Ben.

Patriotic hymns, prayers from the Russian Church, bells ringing – they were almost glad to hear such familiar sounds . . .

Hours passed. The children were less afraid, but they were becoming more aware of how uncomfortable they were: they were cold; the corners of the trunk hurt. They were hungry.

Ben had the idea of opening the trunk; it looked as if it was full of old papers and rags. Feeling about in the dark, they spread them out and made a bed in the trunk where they could finally lie down, groaning, arguing, each one pulling the softest bits of cloth to their own side, leaving the other the newspapers that lined the bottom. It all smelled of dust and moth balls. They couldn't stop sneezing. Finally, they snuggled up to each other. They were safe, they were warm like this, but afraid that the cover might slam shut and suffocate them. They looked at it, straining their eyes in the darkness, and gradually they managed to make out the gleam of the metal fittings.

Outside, the frenzy continued. Suddenly, Ada sat up and shouted in a voice that was unlike her normal voice: it was shriller, deeper, as if someone else was crying out for help through her. 'I can't stand it any more! I'll die if it doesn't stop.'

'It won't stop,' said Ben angrily, 'and I'll tell you something else – you can shout, groan, pray and cry all night long and it won't make a bit of difference!'

'I . . . I don't care,' Ada stammered, sobbing. 'I don't care if I never eat again, if only they would be quiet!'

'And that won't make any of them shut up either,' said Ben.

This seemed so obvious to Ada that she calmed down and suddenly felt quite happy.

'Come on. Let's play.'

'Play what?'

'There's a boat,' said Ada excitedly, 'a boat caught in a storm. Can you hear it? The wind is blowing. The waves are crashing.'

'Yes! And we're pirates,' shouted Ben, jumping up and down on the floor of the trunk, making it creak and groan like the hull of a ship in distress. 'Ship ahoy! Raise the jib, the topsail and the flag! I see land! Land! Land!'

They were happy now. The cold draught that fell against their shoulders was the frosty breath of an iceberg they'd only just missed in the darkness; the creak of the boards, the rags, even the hunger that gnawed at them, all that was no longer reality, but a story, an adventure, a dream. Outside, the screams, the cries for help, the din, the storm sweeping through the old street, they all became the crashing of waves, the roar of the wind, and delighted, they strained to hear the mournful sound of the bells, fragments of prayers that rose towards them as if from some faraway shore.

They reached the height of joy when Ben found in his pocket a box of matches and a piece of a candle, along with a ball of thick string, some bits of bread, a whistle and two nuts he'd forgotten about.

They shared the nuts; they came from the Christmas tree. They were painted gold on the outside, but inside they were dry and bitter. They lit their candle and set it on the edge of the trunk; the tiny little flame that fluttered in the cold air made the attic seem even more like a fantastical world, dark and mysterious, half vision, half game. And so the night passed. Outside, the noise seemed to quieten down, at last. The children, overcome from shouting, from hunger, from the strangeness of it all, suddenly dropped down into the trunk and fell fast asleep.

8

Very early the next morning, the door was opened by Aunt Raissa. At first, she couldn't see the children; she looked anxiously around for them, letting out a cry when they suddenly emerged from the trunk, their clothes all crumpled and dirty, their hair grey with dust. She took hold of their arms and pulled them out of their hiding place.

'You're going to stay with some friends of Lilla,' she said. 'There's no one in the streets now. It's safe to go. You'll sleep there, for one or two nights, maybe.'

The children, half asleep, followed her downstairs. Their hands and feet were frozen. Their bodies felt heavy and painful. They rubbed their little dirt-streaked faces and tried, without success, to force open their eyes: their heavy, burning eyelids shut again almost immediately.

It wasn't until they'd gone past the kitchen that they woke up.

'Can't we have something to eat?'

'You'll eat when you get to Lilla's.'

'But why?'

'We didn't light the fire this morning.'

'Why not?'

Aunt Raissa didn't reply, but while they were getting dressed, she gave them a bit of black bread she'd brought for them. She took it out of a package that also had some clothes in it.

'There's a shirt and a pair of socks for each of you, just in case . . . it goes on for longer . . .'

'Longer than what?'

'Be quiet, Ada! Longer than we think.'

'What do they want to do to us?'

'Nothing. Be quiet.'

'Well, why do we have to go then?'

'Will you shut up, you idiot?' hissed Aunt Raissa, shaking her son by the shoulder.

She cautiously opened the front door. Nastasia was waiting outside.

'Go now, quickly!'

She walked a little way with them. Never had they seen her go out like this, with no hat or coat; it was bitterly cold. Her face was deathly pale and the corners of her mouth were turning blue. For the first time in his life, Ben took his mother's hand and looked at her lovingly.

'Come with us, Mama.'

'I can't. I have to help look after Ada's grandfather.'

'What did they do to him?' asked Ben, as Ada turned pale and looked down at the ground. She didn't know why, but she was afraid to hear the answer.

'Nothing,' replied Aunt Raissa, 'but they threw all his work into the fire. He's beside himself now.'

'But why? How silly,' said Ben, laughing. 'If they'd thrown *him* in the fire, I'd understand, but some old papers!'

'Shut up!' Ada suddenly shouted, tears streaming down her face. 'You don't understand anything, you . . . you . . .'

She couldn't think of anything sufficiently insulting to say. She slapped him across the face and he slapped her back, twice. Aunt Raissa separated them.

'Stop it, both of you! Go with Nastasia! Quickly now!'

She kissed them and left. Nastasia walked swiftly; the children ran alongside her, clinging on to her skirts. They looked around them aghast. Was this really their own street? They didn't recognise it. It seemed entirely different, frightening and strange. The buildings that had three or four floors hadn't been damaged much – a few windows were broken – but the run-down houses, so numerous in the poor neighbourhood, the street stalls, the kosher butchers, the shops with only one room, an attic and a worn-out roof looked as if they'd been ripped out of the ground and thrown on top of each other, as if there had been a cyclone or a flood. Other houses were missing their doors and windows: burnt out and charred by the smoke, they looked dark and menacing. On the ground, bits of metal, tiles, cast iron, wooden planks, bricks lay in chaos – endless debris in which they could make out a boot here, a shattered clay pot there, the handle from a saucepan, and further along, the twisted high heel from a woman's shoe, broken chairs, a nearly new ladle, what used to be a blue earthenware teapot, empty bottles whose necks had been shattered. It had all been left for the looters, but inexplicably certain things had been spared, just as in a fire a fragile piece of furniture sometimes escapes unscathed. All the shops were empty, their windows dark and gaping.

White and grey feathers floated slowly down through the air: torn eiderdowns shed them gently from top windows.

'Faster! Faster!' said Nastasia.

They were afraid of these deserted streets, the dark, ravaged houses.

The lower town was separated from the upper levels by a flight of steps, where women hunched over their baskets and buckets on market days to sell fish, fruit, and wafer-thin, crumbly little croissants dotted with poppy seeds that tasted of water and sand.

The children and Nastasia vaguely hoped they were leaving

the terrifying sight of the pillaged streets behind them, that everything would once again be back to normal as soon as they set foot in the upper town: the colourful sleighs, people calmly walking along, shops full of merchandise. But here, too, it all looked different . . . Perhaps it was because of the early morning light, but everything seemed deathly pale, blurred, as if it were twilight. A few street lights still shone here and there. It was freezing cold with a bitter feel that meant it would soon snow. Ada had never felt so cold, even though she was dressed in warm clothes; for the first time in her life, she found herself outside without having first had some hot tea. The bread was a day old and difficult to swallow; her throat felt sore.

The avenue they were crossing was deserted, the shops barricaded, the windows barred; certain shopkeepers were Jewish; the others feared the riff-raff, the beggars who followed along with the soldiers and pillaged everything, not caring what religion their victims practised. The houses where the Russian Orthodox lived all displayed icons on their balconies, in the hope that respect for the Holy Images would prevent them from being attacked.

The children tried to get Nastasia to talk to them, but she seemed not to hear. She wore the same wooden, bleak, cruel, impassive expression as when Aunt Raissa scolded her for having had a man stay the night, or for burning the roast, or for getting drunk. She wrapped her shawl more tightly under her chin and kept walking without a word.

In front of the church they saw the first human faces; several women stood at the entrance, gazing into the distance and talking excitedly. One of them spotted Nastasia. 'Where are you going?' she shouted.

Nastasia gave the name of the street where Lilla's friends lived.

The women surrounded her, all chattering at once:

'May God protect you! Don't go that way . . . Some drunken Cossacks knocked a woman over and their horses trampled her . . .

She hadn't said a word to anyone, she was just walking past . . .
They rode their horses on to the pavement . . . No, they thought
she was running away: she was carrying a packet of clothes under
her arm and they wanted to have it; she didn't give it up willingly, so . . . No, no! That's nonsense, the horse took fright . . .
She was running across the road and fell . . . Anyway, she's dead
now, don't go that way . . . especially not with the children . . .'

They were tugging at Nastasia's sleeve and skirt. The wind
made their shawls billow around their heads as they huddled
together.

Ada started to cry. One of the women tried to console her,
others kept shouting. Some of them began fighting, hurling insults
and punching each other. Nastasia rushed from one person to
another, then grabbed the children by the hand and ran down the
street, only to hurry back again, moaning: 'What should I do?
Where should I go? Oh, please tell me what to do! . . . They're
ransacking the lower town and here they're killing people . . .
Where should I go? What should I do?'

A woman who had been standing further away suddenly ran
towards them, shouting.

'There they are! They're coming! They're nearly here! They're
drunk! They're trampling everything in their way! Lord Jesus,
have pity on us!'

Some Cossacks on horseback galloped across the street. In the
crush that followed, Ada and Ben got separated from Nastasia.
Without thinking, they threw themselves into a nearby courtyard,
then another, until they reached an alleyway and ended up back on
the main road. They could hear the Cossacks shouting, the horses
whinnying, their hooves beating the frozen ground. The children
were delirious with fear. Blindly they kept running, panting, holding
each other's hand, absolutely convinced that the horde of soldiers
was after them and that they would meet the same fate as the woman
who had been crushed to death a few moments before. Their bulky,

heavy winter coats were slowing them down. Ben had lost his cap; his hair was too long and covered his eyes so he couldn't see anything. Every breath he took felt like a knife ripping into his chest. Ada saw the Cossacks only once. She quickly glanced back and spotted one of them laughing as he rushed forward. A piece of velvet was tied to his saddle; it had unrolled itself and trailed behind him in the melted snow and mud. Ada would never forget the colour of that bit of velvet, a pink that was nearly mauve and shimmered like silver.

It was daylight now. Instinctively the children ran ever higher, up towards the hills, leaving the ghetto far behind them. Finally, they stopped; everything had gone quiet. The Cossacks hadn't followed them, but they were all alone and didn't know where to go.

Ada collapsed on to a stone, sobbing. She had lost her hat, her gloves, her muff; the torn hem of her coat trailed sadly along the ground. She rubbed her face with both hands; her pale little cheeks were splattered with dirt; her tears etched long stripes down her dusty face.

'We'll go back down the hill and try to get to where Lilla's staying,' said Ben, panting.

'No!' cried Ada, shaking like a leaf. 'No! I'm scared! I don't want to! I'm scared!'

'Listen, this is what we're going to do. We're going to go through the courtyards, behind the houses. No one will see us and we won't see anything.'

But Ada just kept on saying 'No! No!' over and over again. She clung on to the stone, as if it were the only safe place in the world.

They had ended up on one of the quietest, wealthiest streets in the city, surrounded by large gardens. Everything exuded peacefulness. No doubt the people who lived here had no idea what was happening down by the river. Not a single Cossack came to disturb their tranquillity; perhaps they looked upon the horror and confusion of the ghetto as if they were at the theatre, with the superficial shudder of spectators watching a drama who quickly reassure themselves with their comfortable sense of security: 'That would never happen to *me*. Never.' They were lucky. A million times luckier than her. And yet, they were Jewish too, just like her, weren't they? Ada imagined them like angels who leaned over the balconies of the heavens and watched the wretched earth with indifference. This was where she wanted to stay – with them. She refused to go back down.

'Let's stay here, Ben,' she pleaded softly.

He got angry, called her 'mad, an idiot, a coward', but she knew very well that he didn't really want to leave this heavenly place either.

They held hands and walked aimlessly along. Ada clung to her cousin's arm, limping. Ben had fallen and torn his trousers, his knee was bleeding.

'Maybe we'll find someone who'll ask us to come inside,' Ada said shyly.

Ben laughed sarcastically. 'Ah, so that's what you think, do you?'

'Ben,' said Ada after a moment, 'this is where the Sinners live.'

'So?'

'So they're our cousins . . .'

'So you think we should go to their house, do you?'

'Why not?'

'They'd chase us away.'

'Why?'

'Because they're rich.'

'But we wouldn't ask them for money!'

Ben called her 'an idiot' again. She didn't argue, just sighed sadly and kept on walking. She could feel Ben beside her, shivering from the cold.

'This is where they live,' said Ada, pointing out the street.

'I don't give a damn.'

But the wind was blowing more harshly now. She took Ben's hand.

'We could at least get out of the cold for a while under their porch. I remember they have a porch with columns and a roof . . . made of marble,' she added, after thinking for a moment.

'Marble?' said Ben, shrugging his shoulders. 'Why not solid gold?' he sniggered.

'Well, anyway, it's a porch and we'd get out of the wind.'

'And how would you get into the garden?'

'I thought you bragged about being able to climb over any gate, even the highest?'

'Well *I* could, maybe . . . but *you*, you're just a girl!'

'I could do it just as well as you,' she said, angrily.

'Really? Just look at yourself! You're a real sight, hobbling about in the snow . . . And we only ran for half an hour!'

'Well, what about you? You were the one who fell down while we were running away, weren't you? Your knee's bleeding.'

'I bet that I'll be able to climb right over the top of the gate and jump down into the garden, and that you won't even make it to the first rung!'

'Well, we'll see about that!'

'I dare you!'

They ran all the way to the Sinners' house. It was already nine o'clock and there was the odd passer-by: a few servants were hurrying towards the shops and the marketplace in the centre of town; a footman was walking some dogs; a worker was sweeping away the snow; but the children chose a moment when there was no one in sight and started to climb over the gate. They were both agile, even though their movements were hindered by their padded winter coats. Ben got over first and gave Ada a scornful look. Ada, putting herself in God's hands – she wouldn't dream of asking her cousin for help – managed to get a foothold between two gilded bars. Getting up was the most important step; you could always get down . . . slowly or fast . . . She jumped down on to the snow-covered lawn and got buried up to her waist. Ben reached out to her; he pushed, pulled, hoisted her up so she was finally standing. Creeping behind the bushes, they made their way to the door, or rather to the front porch with its oval ceiling and slender stone columns. Ben and Ada edged their way along the cold wall and waited . . . for what, they had no idea . . . At first, they were just relieved to be out of the wind, but soon they felt horribly anxious and their exhaustion and hunger were stronger than ever.

'Let's ring the bell,' Ada suggested in a quiet, nervous voice.

Ben, his face turning blue from the cold, shook his head 'no', but less insistently. Ada rang the bell. They huddled together, their hearts racing, staring at the door. It opened. A maid appeared and tried to shoo them away; she was a fat, dark-haired girl, with a little lace bow comically perched above her large, ruddy face with its sullen expression. But Ben had put his hand in the door-frame and was holding it open.

'We want to see Mr Sinner,' Ada said quickly. 'We're cousins of his.'

'What are you talking about?' the maid said, dumbfounded, as she leaned towards Ada.

'We're Mr Sinner's cousins. We wish to speak to him,' Ada said again, this time more confidently.

The maid hesitated. But the children had caught a glimpse of the entrance hall and could already feel its warmth, so were filled with a desperate sort of courage. They pushed the maid aside and walked right past her.

'Very well!' she said. 'I'll let Madame know . . . But you stay right where you are, or else!'

She went out, but they followed close on her heels; they knew very well they would be sent away. They couldn't let their rich relations have any time to think.

In the dining room, where the Sinner family ate breakfast every morning, with its long red damask drapes, its expensive, impressive furniture, there suddenly appeared two pale little urchins with torn clothes and dishevelled hair. They were full of daring, arrogance and fear, yet yearned to be fed, warmed, reassured.

His voice hesitant, Ben began explaining who they were and why they were there. It was a long story. As for Ada, all she could do was stare. She didn't just look at everything around her. She drank it in, as a person dying of thirst pounces upon a drink of water and gulps it down, still not managing to quench his thirst or let go of the glass; this was how each colour, the shape of each object, the faces of these strangers seemed to pierce her, finding their way into a secret place, deep within her heart, a place she had not realised even existed, until now. She stood absolutely still, wide-eyed, and with a wild, stunned expression gazed at the heavy, matt fabric of the red curtains, the high-backed ebony chairs covered in damask, the bright walls painted a pale cream to bring out the richness of the other colours, the deep purple of the carpets, the dark wood of the furniture, the silver platters on the sideboard.

In the middle of the room stood a very large table; some women were sitting around it, and with them, Harry. She recognised him at once. He was wearing a dressing gown of plum-coloured silk. Ada had never seen anything like this shimmering, heavy satin; she thought that Harry must have been ill to be so pampered and dressed like this. In front of him was a porcelain cup, as white and delicate as an egg shell, and a silver egg cup. On a plate sat two pieces of brown bread with butter and jam. One of the women was spreading the bread with butter she took from a small crystal dish with a lid decorated with a silver pine cone. Another woman was pouring Harry some coffee from a silver pot with a very long spout. A third woman added the milk; looking through her lorgnette, she carefully skimmed the cream off the top with a little silver spoon. The fourth woman was cutting up an egg she had just taken out of a bowl, also made of silver, full of boiling hot water. But she didn't cut it up with her knife, as Ada had only ever seen done until now; she used a pair of gilded scissors, made specially to cut eggs, and, to Ada, this was more extraordinary than everything else.

Two of the four women were wearing lace dressing gowns and, despite the fact that it was morning, large diamond earrings. One was Harry's mother, the other, one of his married aunts. They were plump, heavy women, with pale skin and shiny black hair, parted down the middle so it fell in two arcs at the sides of their foreheads. Sitting at the table like two enormous white peonies, they had the replete, lazy, slow-moving demeanour of contented matrons, and the scornful pout and hard, implacable eyes of women who are too rich, too happy. The two younger ones were unmarried aunts; they dressed in the English style — straight skirts in a coarse, masculine material, linen blouses with starched collars, as stiff as a yoke — and had the mannerisms of that younger generation of Jewish millionaires: more 'lady-like' than was natural, with an affectation of simplicity and austerity, as if they wished each of their gestures to say, 'You see how I wish to go unnoticed, *inconspicu-ous* as they say in English. I wish to blend in with mere mortals so they may forget who I really am.'

At the sight of Ben and Ada, everyone stopped eating. Lorgnettes were raised and dropped again. Voices cried out: 'What on earth is going on?'

As Ben started speaking, Harry grew pale and stopped eating. He looked at the messy little boy with his bleeding knees, and the pale little girl whose dishevelled hair was so matted with dust and sweat that it fell in a thick tangle over her eyebrows.

Ben noticed him looking at them and deliberately began to

embellish his story; at first it had been more or less accurate, but now, with exquisite pleasure, he started to add gory details about blood, dead bodies, and at least a dozen disembowelled women. Harry pushed his plate away and stood, white and trembling, behind his seat.

Ben stopped to catch his breath.

'Please,' said Ada weakly, 'can you give us something to eat?'

She started to walk towards the table, but the women all leapt up at once and stood in front of Harry to shield him with their bodies.

'Stop her! She mustn't come near us! They might be dirty. They might be diseased. Don't come any closer, child! Stay where you are. We'll give you something to eat. Dolly, take them into the kitchen.'

'We're not dirty,' cried Ada. 'If you'd spent the whole night hiding in a trunk, your faces would be all dusty and your beautiful dresses would get all torn, too.'

'And I hope it does happen to you one day,' she thought, but she didn't say it.

The maid was ordered to take 'these urchins' into the kitchen, give them some bread and tea and wait for further instructions. Harry, meanwhile, had slipped off his chair and disappeared. The children were being led out when Harry came back, followed by an elderly gentleman who bore a strong resemblance to Ada's grandfather; they could have been brothers. Everyone fell silent. He was the master of the house, Sinner senior, so rich that every Jew imagined only Rothschild surpassed him in status and wealth (Tzar Nicholas II came third).

He had a thin, rough, sallow face, a large, oddly-shaped nose, as if some fist had smashed it in two, a crease down his brow so darkly coloured it looked almost purple (the most definite sign, it was said, that he was being ravaged by cancer), greenish eyes streaked with fine, sinuous red lines, and a piercing, unpleasant expression. But his white beard, his shiny, bald, egg-like head, his supple back, his long, dry fingers with their curved, yellow nails, hard as horn, his sharp, drawling Yiddish accent – all these were familiar to Ben and Ada. This wealthy Sinner looked like the old men in the ghetto, the sellers of second-hand goods, the ironmongers, the shoemakers in their stalls. The children were overwhelmed by respect and admiration as they stood before him, but they weren't afraid.

Once again, it was Ben who recounted their adventures. Ada stood a little to the side; she felt weak and ill and suddenly indifferent to her fate. Nevertheless, it occurred to her that she should probably faint. Whenever a child fainted in books, someone immediately came to her rescue; she was given food; she was put to bed – she quivered with desire at the very idea – a clean, warm bed. She closed her eyes so tightly that her head was suddenly filled with a soft, echoing sound, like the sea. She waited a few moments, but she didn't faint; regretfully, she opened her eyes and found herself leaning against the wall once more, her hands crossed tightly in front of her waist, looking at the people around her. The women seemed terribly angry and upset; they were all talking at once, looking at the children with an expression full of terror, almost hate.

'They're mean,' thought Ada. However, as sometimes happened, she was filled with two different feelings both at once: one was naïve, childlike, and the other more mature, understanding and wise. She felt that two Adas lived within her, and one of them understood why she was being sent away, why they spoke to her with such hostility: the famished children stood before these wealthy Jews as an eternal reminder, a shameful and atrocious memory of what they themselves had once been or might have been. No one dared to add: 'what they could become again some day'.

Ada hid behind the curtain and immediately fell half-asleep.

Every now and again she put her hand into her mouth and gently bit down on it in order to stay awake. Then the silk folds of the curtains would part, her pale, sleepy face would appear, and, thinking no one could see her, she would carefully lean forward and stick out her tongue at the women.

When she was pulled out of her hiding place, she was almost sleepwalking. She and Ben were pushed into an enormous room, which was the elderly Sinner's office; a small table was set up, they were sat down at it and given something to eat. Ada was so exhausted that she couldn't even answer the questions the old man asked her; she couldn't even hear him. Later on, Ben would cruelly tease her about this. As for Ben, he spoke too quickly and too loudly, his little voice shrill and passionate.

'So Israel Sinner is your uncle? I've heard of him. He's an honest Jew.'

The old man had spoken these words slowly, sounding thoughtful and with a hint of pity. When anyone spoke of a Jew from the ghetto as honest, how could you not feel sorry; sorry for the poor man to whom God had forgotten to give sharp teeth and claws so he could defend himself?

'Make sure to tell him to come and see me,' he said. 'He'll make some money.' (He had instructions to pass on to his agents in Kharkov; it wouldn't be a bad idea to entrust them to a discreet, hard-working man who didn't seem overly intelligent.)

He turned away so the children could eat in peace, and walked over to the window; from here, he could see the roofs of the ghetto. It would be interesting, Ada thought vaguely, to know what this old man was thinking as he looked down at that cursed part of town, so close yet so far from where he stood . . . But the thoughts of such a rich man were surely impenetrable to mere mortals, as lofty and strange as the spirits who lived in Heaven. And besides, she was so tired that everything, absolutely everything around her took on the feeling of a dream or feverish delirium. She was only truly aware of the world around her the next day, when she was at Lilla's friend's house. The Sinners had contacted her father and he had taken her and Ben there. She had slept for twenty-four hours.

9

The wealthy Sinner kept his promise and gave his relative the opportunity to be useful to him on a few occasions. The commission he agreed to pay him was minimal, but for a man like Israel Sinner, the very fact that he was being protected by a family from such glittering social circles was enough to raise his status. He was showered with respect: what qualities must he possess to be of service to the king of the upper town?

But then his patron died, and the accountants who were dealing with the enormous estate gave Israel the responsibility of concluding several transactions, which he happily did. Other matters were entrusted to him, more substantial ones. Within two years he had become, if not exactly wealthy, at least comfortably well off. With the Jews, everything happened in leaps and bounds. Happiness and misfortune, prosperity and poverty poured down upon them like rain from the heavens upon cattle. This was what filled them simultaneously with perpetual anxiety and invincible hope.

What was more, something else had happened that allowed Aunt Raissa to realise one of her dreams: grandfather had died. Since the night of the pogrom, he seemed to have been shocked into a sort of stupor. He could barely walk and hardly ate anything;

he soon passed away, and with his death, so did the main reason that the Sinners were forced to live in the lower town.

The family moved higher up, halfway between the top of the hill and the ghetto.

Aunt Raissa was not the kind of woman who rested on her laurels. Now it was essential to take charge of Lilla's education and, most importantly, to have her learn French. At this time, there lived in the city an elderly Parisian woman who gave French lessons to children of the well-to-do classes. She was called Madame Mimi. No one ever found out her surname. She was vivacious, elegantly slim, with bulging eyes and a small hooked nose like the beak of a bird, a bird that was losing its feathers but was still rather charming. She had thin, stiff legs, for she suffered from rheumatism, but that didn't stop her from dancing at the Christmas parties, gracefully raising her taffeta petticoat, which was fashionably longer than her full skirt, or from drinking 'one finger of champagne' to toast the health of her pupils. As well as the French language, she taught them Sully Prudhomme's 'La Petite Tonkinoise' and 'Le Vase brisé'. She had an optimistic, kindly, sweet and joyful outlook on life that the bitter Jews could not manage themselves. She hinted that in St Petersburg, where she had spent her youth, she'd had a secret affair with one of the princes (she then sighed as she mentioned the name of someone who had once been famous). This fact was not at all harmful to her reputation. Quite the contrary: there was no one who did not feel flattered to have someone so well-placed in high society under their roof, a woman about whom one could say with absolute certainty that she knew the correct way to eat asparagus (with a fork or with the fingers) and that she would only teach her pupils the very best French – its terribly difficult pronunciation and its amusing slang.

She quickly became fond of Lilla and Ada.

'Lilla is born to inspire love wherever she goes,' she said.

Then, with a swift, delightful movement of her long, dry fingers, as if she were scattering flowers from a bouquet, she seemed to evoke the spirits of the suitors whom Lilla would encounter on life's journey.

'As for little Ada . . . Ah! She knows her own mind . . . When she gives away her heart, it will be for ever.'

Ada felt flattered: the Frenchwoman's opinions where matters of the heart were concerned were indisputable; she was like a master chef stranded on some deserted island after a shipwreck, enthralling the silent and adoring natives with talk of recipes from his homeland. Madame Mimi was ignorant of and looked down upon anything to do with business, commissions, brokerage or even the hierarchy of quarrels in the town, that is to say, everything that had to do with the daily life of the Sinners and people like them. But when it came to the emotions, she was in her element. It was impossible not to believe her. And Aunt Raissa dreamed of Lilla at the Cannes Flower Festival, on a float decked with blooms, while Ada grew to love more and more a shadow, a ghost: the boy, Harry, whom she hadn't seen again since the day of the pogrom and who lived constantly in her heart.

Ada had only one other passion that rivalled her feelings for Harry: painting. She had always done sketches. But when she was about ten years old, she was given her first set of paints, and began tirelessly to copy the street covered in snow beneath her window, the greyish shades of the March sky and people's faces. Whether it was Nastasia with her frightening, dark little eyes set in her reddish face, or Aunt Raissa, hands on hips, her bodice the shape of a mandolin, or Lilla in a smooth cotton petticoat, or the disdainful, elegant Madame Mimi who looked like an aging wagtail, she found everyone interesting, everyone pleased her. But, mainly, it was Harry's face that she drew, over and over again, just as it was etched in her memory.

She showed her drawings to Madame Mimi, who one day recognised Harry among them.

'I can organise things so you get to play with that little boy,' she said, giving Ada one of her bright, knowing looks.

Ada went pale.

'Do you . . . do you know him then?'

'I've given lessons to his family and have excellent relations with them. So, then, next February . . .'

'February?' Ada repeated, breathless.

'If you come to the party at the Alliance Française with your aunt and cousin, I will introduce you to him.'

Every year, the Alliance Française organised an evening of amateur dramatics, followed by a party; the profits went to charitable causes. The people from the middle town always turned out in force, while those from the upper town sometimes made an appearance. Madame Mimi always took great care over the arrangements for the party.

'Ah!' she sighed. 'Once upon a time, in my beloved Prince's house, I used to give balls where champagne flowed like water, where you could hear polkas and mazurkas playing all through the night, and I would dance, as light as a butterfly . . .'

'But you still dance so well,' said Ada.

Then Madame Mimi delicately lifted the petticoat under her skirt and, standing in front of the wardrobe mirror, danced a step, just one, but with so much grace, so much liveliness, combined with a hint of nostalgic self-mockery, that Ada was enchanted.

'Ah! If only I could paint you just like that! But do you think my aunt will take me as well as Lilla?'

'Of course, of course, I'll make sure of it!'

It was autumn, and the party was to be in February. In February, thought Ada, she would see Harry. He would dance with her, play with her! In his eyes, she would no longer be that beggar girl, that vagabond, that outcast, that little Jewish girl from the ghetto.

She could speak French now, she knew how to curtsey; she was 'like the others'. Though she barely knew him, he was more real to her than Ben or Aunt Raissa. As she hurried home from school along the dark, wintry streets, blowing on her fingers, feeling the icy wind and snow burning her eyelashes, she could almost sense the presence of the young boy beside her; she would talk to him and make up what he said in reply. Over and over in her mind, she played out a drama full of surprises and delights, encounters, quarrels, reconciliations.

The day of the party finally arrived. Since morning, certain smells had filled the Sinner household: irons heating in the kitchen, the aroma of little bottles of inexpensive perfume that Lilla had opened, sniffed and nervously compared. Lilla and Ada had laid out their black tights, starched petticoats and Lilla's new grey twill bodice on the bed. Lilla was going to be dancing, singing and reciting in an entertainment called 'The Rose and the Butterfly', especially composed for the occasion by Madame Mimi: Madame had many talents.

'I will appear on stage,' said Lilla, 'and everyone will applaud me.'

She began twirling round and round with joy. She was extremely light and graceful; she had tiny little feet and the kind of legs that were admired in those pre-war days, with a delicate ankle, firm calves and full thighs.

She was in the bedroom with Aunt Raissa and Ada. Ada had grown a lot: her wild hair was brushed back into a short, thick plait, but on her forehead she had kept the uneven fringe that came down over her eyebrows and sometimes fell into her eyes; when that happened, she had the wild, intense look of some little animal hiding in a thicket.

The day passed slowly. Finally, the lamps were lit and the house was filled with the smell of red cabbage cooking for the evening meal, which gave off an even stronger odour than the curling irons.

In the dining room, Ben was entertaining a friend, a little boy from school named Ivanov, with whom he had formed an unusual friendship. Ivanov was eleven years old, with blond hair, a rosy complexion and the ruddy, soft cheeks of a baby. His friends liked to pinch him; wherever they had touched him, there remained a mark as white as snow, while the rest of his face turned so red that his flesh seemed covered in cherries and milk. The two children were sitting in the dining room, beneath the lamp. Little Ivanov, sweet and smiling, with his big blue eyes and plump little red mouth, was listening to Ben's endless talk. He spoke quietly for fear of being overheard by his mother, but the constant movement of his body, his expressive face and gesturing hands were more eloquent than his voice.

He was telling some wild story, a tissue of lies, the tale of a battle he claimed he'd fought, him alone against six boys who were older and stronger than him, who were throwing stones. He described the scene as if he were reliving it: he mimed every detail; he swore by everything that was holy that each and every word was true; he was carried away by his mad inventions; he believed everything he was saying; he could feel his body going hot and cold in turn; he wanted to hug little Ivanov and beat him up, both at the same time, while Ivanov, his head propped up in his hands, seemed to drink in his words, nevertheless asking from time to time:

'That can't be true? Can it? Come on, tell the truth. Is that true?'

'Yes, I swear! May God strike me down! May I die at this very moment if I'm lying! And then a stone hit me right here . . .'

He pointed to the arch of his eyebrow, pushing back the hair that fell on to his face with his feverish little hands. Little Ivanov couldn't help himself repeating over and over again, like an incantation: 'He's lying. This story can't be true. I know it's not true. He's a little Jewish liar. If he'd really been hit in the head with a stone, I'd see a mark.' But wasn't there actually a mark? By rubbing his forehead and pulling his curls back and forth, Ben had managed to create a red patch just above his eye.

'Can you see it? There, can you see it?'

Why was he so determined to lie? To show off to Ivanov, of course, because he liked him. It was only Ivanov's affection and respect that quenched an avid thirst in Ben's soul, a thirst of which he was barely aware.

'And so, you see, Ivanov, you see how I'd be able to stand up for you ... You've got nothing to be afraid of if I'm with you. I'm stronger and smarter than Yatsovlev or Pavlov (they were his rivals). Listen to me, Ivanov, why do you play with them? When spring comes, we'll escape out of the window when everyone's asleep, and we'll light a log at the river's edge, and I'll teach you how to catch fish at night, by torchlight. One of us holds the lit torch,' he said, getting carried away by his fantasies, 'while the sparks fly into the air and singe your hair, and the other one throws in the fishing line, and every time, an enormous silvery fish will leap out, gasping for air, its gills still all red! All you have to do is pick them up with your bare hands. In the morning, we can sell them at the market. After a while, we'll have enough money to buy a gun and real bullets, or even ...'

He added, as if in a dream, 'a bicycle ...'

And his little hands, which had been burning hot, turned icy with desire.

'Will you come with me, Ivanov?'

'Yes.'

'But if I'm going to take you with me, first I have to be sure you'd rather be with me than with Yatsovlev or Pavlov.'

'I would.'

'It's not enough to just say it. From now on, you must avoid them. You can't play with them any more. They're clumsy and mean and stupid. What could you do with them?'

THE DOGS AND THE WOLVES

'I can't promise that . . .'

'Fine then! I won't ask you to do a thing. I'll find myself another friend.'

'But why can't I be friends with you and with them?' exclaimed Ivanov in despair.

'That's impossible,' Ben said coldly. 'You're either with me or against me. Choose. Choose,' he said again, leaning in so close to Ivanov that his black curls were practically touching the other boy's pink knees.

And beneath Ben's glittering, imperious gaze, little Ivanov felt uncomfortable, awkward and impatient.

'I've chosen.'

'Just me then?'

'Just you.'

Ben fell back into his chair. He had got what he wanted, or, at least, the symbol, the image of what he wanted, for the truth was less important to him than the illusion of having obtained what he desired, even for a moment. Now, something more was needed: he would have to bring Yatsovlev and Pavlov under his spell, as well as the Natural Sciences teacher who couldn't stand him, and, finally, Ada, the rebellious Ada, who always stood up to him, challenging him with her bitter mockery, but she . . . Ah! How he longed for the day when he would get his own back on Harry! She never spoke of Harry, but Ben knew that she thought about, and dreamt about, that horrible rich kid. She'd see him tonight . . . That was why Ben had refused to go with his mother and sister to the party. Whenever he thought of Harry, he felt something more subtle, more sophisticated than simple hatred, the kind of feeling you have for a friend who has beaten you up or told on you to the teacher. It was a combination of admiration, envy and fierce repugnance. The fact that Ivanov might have a life that was different from Ben's was in the natural order of things, but Harry . . . 'He could be me, and I could be him,' he thought. He would have liked to see Harry suffer all the things he had suffered: frostbite, feet shredded by shoes that were too tight, the slaps he got from his mother, the slights from his teachers . . . And, at the same time, in his imagination, he took Harry's place. In his mind, he was the one who was well fed, well dressed, loved like Harry. Rich like him. His mother and uncle were definitely right: for a Jew, the only salvation was wealth. He and Harry . . . they were from the same bloodline, shared the same name . . . and yet *he* was always pampered, while Ben . . .

Meanwhile, the girls were getting ready for the party. Lilla had a starched white cotton dress, a moiré silk belt, bronze slippers and a crown of artificial flowers on her head: for a week now, Lilla and Ada had cut out, sewed and arranged tulle forget-me-nots on wire stems. Over her school uniform, Ada wore her best white pinafore; she had a large red ribbon in her hair.

Lilla sprinkled a few drops of perfume on her handkerchief and belt, then moistened her finger with the perfume and rubbed it on her neck and upper lip. Ada looked at her in astonishment.

'Why are you doing that?'

'Ah, well . . .'

'Oh Lilla! Do you think you'll be getting kissed? On the lips? . . . And even on your neck? . . . Oh!'

'Shush! Be quiet! Mama's coming!'

'Give me a little, will you?'

'Why?' said Lilla, smiling at her little cousin. 'Are you also hoping that someone will kiss you, you little brat?'

As a joke, she sprinkled some perfume in Ada's hair. Ada couldn't say a word, she was too deeply moved to laugh along with Lilla. Why was a kiss so forbidden, so desired? She certainly wouldn't get any pleasure at all from kissing Ben! But if she really became Harry's friend, he would kiss her, wouldn't he? She didn't understand why, but alternating waves of hot and cold rushed through her at the thought.

She made a hasty escape, rushing to hide in the junk room; it was dark and smelled musty. She locked the door, got down on her knees in the middle of the room, folded her hands and began praying to God:

'Please make him see me. Please make him notice me.'

She hesitated. Nastasia finished her prayers by making the sign of the Cross, but surely that would be sacrilegious for her? Still . . . she couldn't resist: she traced the sign on her forehead and chest, her hand trembling. She stood up. As she was leaving the junk room, she realised with dismay that her dress had got dirty and her pinafore wrinkled at the knees. But there was nothing to be done.

She sat down beside Lilla and watched her finish getting ready without saying a word. Then Aunt Raissa came to fetch them. She was wearing a purple silk dress and a paste butterfly in her red curls. She puffed up the sleeves of her dress, full of hope.

10

The large hall where the party was being held was decorated with paper garlands, green plants and little French flags. The entertainment had just begun. The sound of rows of chairs creaking under the weight of nervous mothers had ceased; the women sat very still, their lorgnettes fixed on the stage, where a chorus of twenty-five little girls were singing:

'*There is a bird that comes from Fra-a-ance* . . .'

Their mothers had thick necks, wore their hair in large black buns and had diamond earrings whose lustre depended on the rank and social status of their husbands. Anyone wearing a pearl necklace whose husband was not at least a banker would have been considered impertinent, but diamonds were acceptable, even amongst the lowest of the low: the merchants of the Second Guild. And Aunt Raissa had at last taken her place amongst these respected matrons. All of them, however, were seated below a little platform that formed a box reserved for the rich Sinner family.

The wealthy Sinners arrived in the middle of the entertainment. On seeing them enter the room, everyone looked simultaneously flattered and indifferent. It was a great honour to be in the company of the Sinners, but, all the same, they shouldn't forget who they themselves were: the Levys, the Rabinovitches! Every woman puffed up her chest and made her diamonds sparkle, all the while whispering, 'They say the Governor General himself attends their balls . . .'

Harry sat in the middle. He was thirteen years old. Ada would not have been at all surprised if he had been wearing a suit of gold. His clothing was more modest than that, but just as extraordinary in Ada's eyes. He had on trousers the colour of grey pearl, a black jacket and the round collar that boys from Eton wore. He looked shy and sullen, but to Ada, that only added to his prestige. His hair was so beautiful! He was holding one of the programmes designed by Ada, and had a box of chocolates open in front of him. As he took one, he dropped the programme, which fluttered through the air for a moment before landing near Ada. She picked it up and held it tightly in her trembling hand.

Meanwhile, a little girl with hair as curly as a poodle's was reciting Camille's speech in which she curses Rome, generously adding three 'r's to each one that Corneille had written. The audience listened, impressed:

'Rrrome, the unique object of my rrresentment!'

A fat boy with pink thighs came on stage.

'Poordriedoutleafdetachedfromitsstem . . .' he began.

Then he stopped, dissolved in tears and disappeared as if he'd fallen through a trap door.

Next came the dance of 'The Butterfly and the Rose'. Amongst the heavy young girls who surrounded her, Lilla danced with graceful beauty: she waved many multicoloured scarves and smiled at everyone with a tender look that seemed to say, 'How can you not love me? You must love me.'

It was more than a success. It was a triumph. Aunt Raissa sat very tall in her chair, her lips pursed in a contemptuous smile, savouring her pleasure and all the while thinking, 'And you imagine I'm going to let her wither and die in this provincial town as I have, wasting my strength and my talents looking for a husband who might be acceptable? Oh, no. Lilla deserves more than that. You good people will be hearing more about Lilla, and her mother!'

After all, who was that great tragic actress, Rachel? A little Jewish girl, born in a caravan. Nothing was impossible to the Jews. Every path was open to them. They could climb to dizzying heights. All of Mother Russia herself was not a sufficiently brilliant or vast stage for Lilla. (Besides, Moscow and St Petersburg were off limits to Jews.) No, she needed Paris. Only in Paris was it worth trying her luck, risking everything. What a wonderful child she was! How gracefully she bowed as everyone applauded! She was born to be on the stage. The auditorium resounded with shouts of 'Bravo' as she took her final bow and left, her pink and green scarves floating behind her.

Afterwards, dances and games were organised. Harry remained standing next to one of his aunts, rather aloof. Madame Mimi came to fetch Ada. Together they crossed the entire length of the hall, and everyone could see that little Ada Sinner was going to be introduced to her rich cousin. It surprised no one that, even though the two children were closely related, the distance between them was immense. On one side there was money and the uncles who were bankers in Paris; on the other was the ghetto, a lack of education, poverty . . . It was no doubt rather shocking to them that Madame Mimi was behaving this way. These French . . .

Madame Mimi waved at Harry.

'My dear Harry, here is a lovely little girl who would like to meet you. You can dance with her. They're about to play a very pretty waltz.'

Harry raised his eyes and recognised the child he had seen two years before, covered in dust, her hair dishevelled, her hands scratched. She surged up out of a horrible, sordid world, a world of dirt, sweat and blood, far removed yet, despite everything, mysteriously, terrifyingly linked to him. His entire body bristled as if he were a little dog in a forest who was well fed and cared for and who hears the hungry cry of the wolves, his savage brothers. He took a quick step backwards.

'No. I don't dance. No.'

But at the same time, he was dying of shame. He recalled the harshness, the haughtiness with which those children had been treated. He knew very well that, later, he would be sick with remorse over his behaviour: he had a sensitive, moral soul, but he would rather have shaken the hand of the most filthy beggar than this little girl's hand. If he was trembling as he stood opposite her, it was not because she represented poverty to him, but because she represented unhappiness: a kind of unhappiness that was strangely, terrifyingly contagious, the way diseases can be contagious.

'Well, don't dance then!' Madame Mimi urged him on. 'Run off and play together.'

'Madame Mimi,' Harry murmured, 'I just can't.'

'But why not?'

'You know very well . . .'

What could he say, what excuse could he find to make her go away more quickly, so he wouldn't have to see those anxious eyes looking up at him?

'You know that I am not allowed to play with other children,' he said finally.

At that instant, extreme hatred and extreme love merged in Ada's heart, creating a feeling so violent, so contradictory, so upsetting, that she felt as if she had been wrenched in two.

But Harry's emotions weren't simple either: he was afraid of Ada and attracted to her at the same time. He looked at her with passionate, sad curiosity. For a second, his attraction to her was so strong that he said, 'I'm very sorry . . .'

He had gone all red; his little yellowish face, so like Ben's, was now purple. His eyes filled with tears, and when she saw his expression, Ada no longer felt anything but love.

Madame Mimi hurriedly turned and walked away, followed by the little girl, her head lowered. It seemed to Ada that everyone was looking at her and mocking her. Her face took on an expression of such intense seriousness and pain that Madame Mimi stopped when she noticed it.

'Ada,' she said, 'you mustn't want things so badly.'

'I can't help it, Madame,' she replied.

'You must keep more detachment in your heart. Treat life as if you are someone who lends money generously and not a greedy usurer.'

'I can't help it,' she said again.

She was walking but saw nothing. Madame Mimi stopped some children who were playing to suggest they include Ada, but all the teams had already been decided; they refused to let her join in Blind Man's Bluff; no one wanted her for Hopscotch or Musical Chairs. Finally, they let her play a game of Tag. She was caught almost immediately. Never again would she feel such intense distress as at that moment: surrounded by a circle of curious, mocking faces, she ran from side to side, trying to catch the little girls who squealed as they got away.

11

It was nearly midnight, but Aunt Raissa and Madame Mimi were so excited by the success of the party that they didn't want to say goodnight. The Frenchwoman accepted an invitation to the Sinners' to have a cup of tea. Lilla was soon in bed and fast asleep, only her black plait peeking out over the sheets. Ada undressed slowly, her fingers shaking and cold. She got into bed but couldn't go to sleep. On the other side of the wall, Aunt Raissa and Madame Mimi were talking, and Ada could hear every word.

'She instinctively knows how to carry off what she's wearing,' said Madame Mimi.

They were talking about Lilla. Ada felt no jealousy; it was impossible not to be happy for Lilla's good fortune. But, in spite of herself, she lay in the darkness and cried.

'It's sinful to keep that child here . . .'

'Oh, my dear Madame Mimi, you've read my mind! What will she do in such an uncivilised place?'

'She could be one of the belles of Paris in five or six years . . . She'd need some elocution lessons, a few deportment classes . . . The Conservatoire . . .'

At those magical words, Aunt Raissa let out a little strangled cry of desire and regret.

'The Conservatoire, do you really think so?'

'She has such a pretty voice . . .'

'She's a silly little goose,' Aunt Raissa suddenly said with extraordinary bitterness. 'You have to keep an eye on her every minute so she doesn't fall in love with the first good-looking beast who comes along. That's why I could never send her to Paris alone. She'd get distracted.' (What she really meant was 'She'd let herself be seduced by some penniless boy'.)

'Why don't you go and live there? Everyone, no matter what age, should know what it's like to leave your country, to live your life on the throw of the dice. I, for example . . .'

'But *I'm* dependent on someone else. I'm just a poor widow. Someone else supports me,' said Aunt Raissa, irritated.

Never had Ada heard her aunt speak in such a sincere tone of voice. Everything the elderly woman had ever wanted, everything she had ever dreamed of, everything that had remained secret within her for all those long years now escaped as sighs, stifled cries and tears.

'It's so awful not being rich and free! When I think of the Sinners . . . Didn't you tell me that they're leaving Russia to go and live in Europe? That the little boy will be brought up in Paris? What a wonderful future, and how unfair to my family! I'll have to stay here, wasting away from the boredom and mediocrity and imagining the same fate for my daughter. I wasn't made for this kind of life, Madame Mimi. You understand me; you're the only one who understands me . . .'

'Your brother-in-law . . .'

'Israel is so afraid, so cowardly. God, men are such cowards! He would never agree to leave the country. And he'd never send us there. If Lilla were his daughter, but she's only his niece . . .'

'I could offer to take her to live with me . . .'

'With you, Madame?'

'Oh, yes. I inherited a modest amount of money which I've

invested in Russian Bonds. That way, my future is secure. I intend to go back and live in Paris next spring. But I wouldn't dare take on the responsibility of looking after Lilla all by myself . . . Such a young, pretty girl, you understand . . . That would be asking for trouble . . . Only a mother . . .'

'Of course, yes, of course,' Aunt Raissa repeated, lost in thought and secret calculations. 'If it were a matter of his own daughter, I could make Israel see reason . . .'

Suddenly, the two women lowered their voices and Ada couldn't hear anything more. They whispered for a long time, then Madame Mimi exclaimed, 'It's very true that the child is gifted . . . And she has a unique character, very endearing . . .'

'Yes, she could study in Paris, yes, that's for sure . . .'

Ada sat up in bed, her heart pounding. Was it possible, was it even conceivable that they were talking about her?

'He adores his daughter,' Aunt Raissa was saying. 'He would make any sacrifice for her. He would be so happy to help her become an artist. Ah, if only my poor Lilla still had a father! . . . But that's life. You have to take what it gives you.'

'You could find a place to live near me.'

'Do you know many people there, Madame Mimi?'

'I used to know a lot of people,' said the old woman.

She paused for a moment, then continued in a voice that was artificially light and gay, the voice you use to forget your sorrows, the way you sing when you want to boost your courage.

'I knew everyone in Paris, in the past. I was called . . . Don't tell anyone now, it was my nickname, my *nom de guerre* . . . Yes, I was part of a very élite clique, very talented, where everyone had a little nickname . . . I was called "Wild Card" because I loved to play . . . All that was a very long time ago, but I've kept . . . I surely must have kept some loyal, influential friends . . .'

She fell silent. All Ada heard for a while was the sound of teaspoons stirring cups of tea.

What images were conjured up in Aunt Raissa's mind? It was quite possible that she was confusing Lilla with herself when she was young, confusing Lilla's destiny with her own . . . Never had she loved her daughter so deeply. She even had a bit of tenderness left over for other people.

'It would be such a shame not to try to cultivate my niece's gifts,' she said warmly, speaking of Ada. 'She could become a great artist. I'll speak to her father about it first thing tomorrow.'

12

It is characteristic of the Jewish way of thinking that if it had been a question of sending Lilla and Ada away to be educated in order that they might end up in a safe, ordinary profession, as a seamstress or an accountant, Israel would have hesitated for a long time and, in the end, would not have agreed to let the children go. Their leaving would turn his world upside down and increase his expenses. And, of course, he would lose his daughter. Paris was far away, travel was expensive, he couldn't even hope to see her again for two or three years . . . But this was not a matter of a safe, ordinary profession. It was not a question of logic, but of a dream. Leaving was a leap into the unknown. They would either lose everything or make a fabulous fortune. Ada might become a famous painter and Lilla a great actress. Who could know what God had in store for them? It would be extremely expensive, of course, but what wouldn't he have done for his daughter, his own flesh and blood? He felt vaguely guilty where Ada was concerned: she could have been happier . . . It wasn't his fault, poor man, that her mother had died so young; he wasn't responsible for Aunt Raissa's temperament, or Ben's devilishness . . . But, in spite of himself, he always wanted to ask Ada's forgiveness for bringing her into the world. It wasn't a very nice gift . . . He could at least let her try her luck, give her a chance of happiness . . .

He agreed to allow Aunt Raissa and the three children to leave. In Russia, without the watchful eye of his mother, Ben would come to no good, and Russia was not the ideal country for a little Jewish boy . . . Soon they would have to deal with the problem of choosing a career for him, of military service (that endless nightmare), of getting him into university . . . It was better for Ben to leave as well.

One spring morning, Israel watched them climb on to the train, loaded down with trunks, food and even some furniture.

It was May 1914.

For the first two years of the war, Israel regularly sent them money to live on. They had rented an apartment in Paris with Madame Mimi and shared the cost. It wasn't exactly what Madame Mimi had led them to expect . . . The elderly lady had not been able to contact many of her old friends; she didn't know why. Some had died, others moved away. Some of them didn't seem to remember her. Besides, it was wartime . . .

For two years, the life of the Sinners and Madame Mimi was calm, mediocre, melancholy. Then the Revolution swept through Russia, dragging along everything in its wake and then destroying it all, including, with a great deal of other debris, the life, the destiny and even the memory of Israel Sinner.

With no further rent payments coming from Russia, their State Bonds now worthless, Aunt Raissa revealed what she herself had always known: she was no ordinary soul. With the little money she had managed to save, she bought some cloth patterns and two tailor's dummies; she taught her daughter and her niece how to cut fabric, and, by stealth and by force, wrenched from Madame Mimi the few valuables she had left – some jewellery, gifts from the Prince and mementos from happier times – and she became a seamstress.

If there was anything presumptuous about a poor Jewess from an isolated province in the Ukraine selling dresses to Parisian ladies, she dismissed the thought.

They sublet Madame Mimi's apartment and found a small three-bedroom flat in the Ternes area, where the bourgeoisie and the upper classes crossed paths and often merged, like two tributaries of the same river.

Their furnished apartment smelled of dust and that unique odour found only on the premises of inexpensive dressmakers: cooking, wool and the cheap, strong perfume the clients wore. The windows were rarely opened: both Aunt Raissa and Madame Mimi feared fresh air. Lilla got a job at a music hall, Ben delivered the dresses to the clients, while Ada was used by her aunt for all sorts of jobs: sewing, collecting up the pins, measuring the ladies, copying the patterns that they secretly stole. She was given food and lodging, and showered with abuse. Aunt Raissa had never spared Ada her criticism, but it became more and more bitter with each passing day. Not only because Ada was now her financial responsibility, but because, without realising it, she was a constant reminder to the elderly woman of how Lilla had come down in the world; her Lilla, in whom she had placed so much hope and who was now only just good enough to parade naked on a music hall stage, Lilla, who was letting herself lose her youth, her beauty, and who couldn't even manage to find a rich lover! Men all fell in love with Lilla, but through a kind of mocking twist of fate, she only met the poor ones: married, petit-bourgeois men, cautious and mean with money, or second-rate opportunists.

When Ada was fifteen and had become pretty, her aunt felt a deep loathing for her. Ada responded by being insolent: since childhood, this had been her most powerful weapon. It was a strange fact that the old woman's anger only cooled when Ada replied with the most insolent, witty retort she could think of. Aunt Raissa wouldn't let it rest, however. She'd always had a sharp tongue and she was grateful to her niece for giving her a chance to use it, just as a professional duellist enjoys facing a worthy opponent on the field of battle. Unfortunately, she had one fault that was common in women: she loved winning. She caused endless scenes and, endowed with an implacable memory, she never let go of former grudges when new ones arose, thus tirelessly repeating and embellishing the same issues, varying her arguments in a fashion that was truly creative. She was like a wasp who sinks its sting into you, but then continues to buzz around you.

Her niece stood up to her, but increasingly Ada took refuge within herself; her imagination was so fertile and strange that nothing could really offend or hurt her. When Aunt Raissa began swearing at her, Ada managed, through sheer force of will, to look at her aunt's harsh, intelligent, bitter face, not as an ill-treated young girl would, but with the eye of a painter. Afterwards, she would take a page from her sketchbook and reproduce the features etched in her memory.

Sometimes, she would intentionally annoy her aunt in order to get another look at the little wrinkle at the corner of her mouth that only appeared when she was extremely angry. That cruel, sardonic expression fascinated her: it surfaced and disappeared like a serpent's tail twitching in the grass; it was impossible to catch. It both terrified and thrilled her in a unique way. The outside world was full of shapes and colours that were impossible to remember for ever, constantly lost, but seeking them out, pursuing them, was the most precious thing on earth.

'You live in a dream-world,' said Lilla. 'You're nearly sixteen years old and you act as if you're twelve. You draw and nothing else matters; you're wasting the best years of your life,' she added.

They were leaning against the narrow window ledge in the attic, up above the street. It was a hot evening, too oppressive for the beginning of spring. The sound of crying children was heard on every floor. Ada thought she would try to paint this wide avenue, the way the evening shadows were interspersed by flashes of light, the stormy sky that seemed to crackle with sparks, the flower seller with her red hair tied up in a bun, and that woman dressed in mourning clothes walking beneath the street lamps who looked up now and again, as if she were suffocating and needed air; her distraught face seemed made of white lead beneath the light.

Lilla stretched languidly. 'Haven't you ever met a man you found attractive?' she asked.

What? What was Lilla saying? Hadn't she, Ada, ever met . . . ? No. No. She shook her head, proud and defiant. She was destined for an existence that was different from Lilla's; she was destined for other pleasures, emotions that no one could understand or share. And yet . . . for a fifteen-year-old girl, certain words spoken in her presence (*a man, attractive* . . .) are like refrains from within, murmured by a voice inside her, calling up a muffled, almost threatening echo.

Madame Mimi was in the room. Her hair was white, but she still stood tall on her delicate legs; her hands were knotted and deformed by rheumatism, but she still had a keen eye.

'Ada is still thinking about that little Harry Sinner,' she said.

'No, Madame Mimi!' cried Ada.

Lilla laughed. Aunt Raissa sniggered.

'That's her all over,' Ben groaned with scorn.

'You still think about him, Ada. You'll never forget him,' Madame Mimi said once more, her voice low and mocking. It was the voice of an elderly seer, the tone she used when speaking of love, as if only then some chord vibrated within her, one musical note still alive amongst all the others that time had all but destroyed.

'You know that we're neighbours, don't you?' Lilla whispered in her ear.

'Neighbours?'

'I mean, they live quite near us, on the other side of l'Étoile, on the Rue des Belles-Feuilles, number 40. I happened to notice it in the telephone directory.'

Instinctively, Ada leaned out of the window and looked at the avenue that led to the Place de l'Étoile. It was strange to think that he was closer to her here in Paris than in their home-town, where they had been separated by the lower town, the long boulevard lined with poplar trees, and the hills.

They were all laughing, and she was ashamed at feeling her former passion rise within her.

'It's not my fault,' she thought. 'It's because I just can't forget certain faces once I've seen them, or certain houses, or certain sights. *They're* indifferent or fickle because they remember nothing. But I can't forget, I can't. It's a unique curse that makes me recall every feature, every word, every moment of joy or pain once they have struck me. One day, I'll go and see the house where he lives.'

Months went by, however, and still she couldn't bring herself to go. What good would it do? It was so childish . . . Most impor-tantly, she mustn't find more ways to feed a dream that was gradually becoming less damaging, only half real, half imagination. As she grew up, she had become more and more distanced from it, just as you forget a book you read and loved passionately when you were a child. You may still love it, but back then, you believed in it. Now you realise that it was nothing but poetry, fiction, an illusion, less than nothing . . . Nevertheless, she had to avoid recalling anything from behind the door she had closed for ever, be careful not to remember any concrete details – the shape of a face, a voice, a look that might suddenly recreate the dream, give it the depth, the force, the taste of reality. And so, nearly two years passed.

13

One day, Ada went to the Rue des Belles-Feuilles to deliver a dress. As she was coming back, she walked slowly, hesitantly, towards number 40, only a few steps away. Good Lord, why not? It was an innocent pleasure, and she had very few pleasures at all. Since chance had brought her so close to the one she had loved throughout her childhood (she realised now the absurd and un-wavering nature of her feelings, which really were similar to love), why not get closer, look at the house, risk catching a glimpse of Harry? She walked slowly on, her heart pounding. Then she saw a grand house; it was not particularly large and had a stone balcony that ran beneath three high French windows. She vaguely remem-bered a painting from the French School in which windows like these opened out on to gardens in which women in pale-pink crinoline dresses danced in a pavilion with black and white paving stones.

And then, as if to complete the analogy, some young men and women came out on to the balcony and stood beneath the beauti-ful, leafy June trees that framed the house; she could hear an orchestra playing in the background, the joyous, soft sounds of a party. It was the time of year when balls and afternoon dances were held. Yes, they were dancing, having fun: she could see couples through the open windows, others leaning against the balcony. Here was an entire world of pleasure and refinement that was foreign to her, a world she had never even dreamed of because it was so distant from her, so strange. How happy those young women were! It was getting late, nearly seven o'clock, and the light was particularly soft and pale, melting into the clear, warm dusk. Which one of the boys was Harry? Impossible to recognise him. She looked for the most handsome, the one with the best physique, and called him Harry in her heart.

One of the young girls leaned out over the balcony, dangling streamers over the edge. Ada was fascinated by the colour of her dress: green and silver. It was hot; Ada was thirsty and her mouth burned from the dust; she'd been walking for a long time. That colour – greenish water beneath a carpet of young leaves drenched in rain – quenched her thirst. She admired the beauty and happiness of those young women, but she didn't envy them any more than she might envy the figures in a painting. Quite the contrary: she was grateful to them for giving her a little taste of the party, the music, the smiles, the luminosity of their fair hair in the June light.

'I'd like to paint this,' she thought. 'It's not exactly my style . . . I prefer darker, more squalid scenes, but perhaps just once . . . those dresses the colour of flowers, dusk in summer, and the clear light, so pale against the trees . . . It's all so beautiful!'

From her bag she took out the sketchbook and worn-down pencil she always had with her and quickly drew the pose of the young woman with the ribbons leaning over the balustrade. Behind her stood a young man, watching her. Was it Harry? Could it perhaps really be Harry? Near to Ada stood a group of chauffeurs who were also watching the dancers. They seemed only vaguely interested and looked slightly disapproving, the way that servants look upon their masters' follies. She turned towards them and asked quickly, 'Excuse me, does this house belong to the Sinners?'

Her heart was pounding. She wasn't mistaken. This was Harry's parents' house.

'Isn't their son called Harry?' she said.

'That one?' one of them replied, pointing to the young man on the balcony. 'Yes, that's him, that's their son.'

She drank him in with her eyes, studied him with the deep, piercing gaze of a painter. He had dark hair, a finely chiselled face, alive and mocking, a thin nose and long neck. She was struck once again by his resemblance to Ben.

'The classic Jewish man,' she thought, 'slight, intelligent and sad. Did these rosy-skinned, blonde girls find him attractive? Alas! That wasn't the question; the question was whom *he* might find attractive . . .'

Suddenly, she closed her eyes, in the grip of a kind of dream, a fantasy, as she called it, in which scenes created in her mind became as clear and real as life itself.

She could see herself as a child, the day she went to Harry's house. She imagined a different Ada, a more courageous one; she should have walked up to him and taken his hand. She didn't know why, but she was certain he would have gone with her . . . And as for all those women jabbering around him . . . so what! Who cared about them? He would have gone with her.

'I'll never love anyone but you,' she thought with a feeling of despair, the feeling you get when you realise you're destined for poverty and unhappiness. 'Even if I spend my whole life in Aunt Raissa's workshop, become an old woman without ever saying a single word to you, or even end up marrying someone else, I'll never forget you. I'll never stop loving you, never. I'm more sure of that than of my life itself!'

She looked down at her dusty shoes with their misshapen heels, at her hands covered in pin pricks, and the bitter irony of her situation washed over her.

'Dante and Beatrice,' she thought. 'How people would laugh

if they knew! But surely everyone carries such mad dreams deep within themselves . . . Or perhaps only the Jews are like that? We are such a hungry race, starving for so long that reality is not enough to satisfy us. We must have the impossible. And what about Harry? What does he desire? Something better than what he has, without a doubt, just as I do now? Something so vast, such an abundance of happiness that nothing can possibly satisfy him.' She suddenly thought: 'Oh! It's so late. Aunt Raissa will make a fuss. But it's so difficult to leave. They're dancing again, so graceful, so carefree . . . Some servants are carrying platters . . . I bet they're having ice cream . . . How wonderful to eat an ice cream on a hot evening like tonight . . . But I have to go. Adieu, Harry . . .'

14

She opened the door quietly, hoping to get inside without being seen, but Aunt Raissa started screaming at her the minute she walked into the hallway.

'So it's you! You've deigned to come back? You've deigned to remember that it's eight o'clock and that you left at six? Do I feed you so you can go for a stroll like a princess? I thought you were dead, run over! Not that I would have shed any tears over you . . . Well, where were you? Who were you roaming around with?'

'I went for a walk. Alone.'

'Alone? I know you girls!'

'You know your girl!'

'Do you want a slap?' Aunt Raissa hissed.

Her thin, hard hands often slapped them, and while Ada and Lilla didn't like it, they put up with it without rebelling, just as you put up with bad weather. But the contrast now between the scene that Ada had witnessed a few moments before and this shouting, her threats, her brutality . . . It was too painful, too sinister . . .

'I'm not eight years old any more,' she said. 'I'm stronger than you. I'll hit back!'

Aunt Raissa drew back.

'Give me the money for the dress. They paid you, didn't they?'

'Yes, of course they paid me. Here's your money . . . here . . .'

She stopped dead, terrified. She realised that she didn't have her bag. And the eight hundred francs paid by the client for the dress she'd delivered? What had happened to it? Had she dropped her bag in the street while hurrying, or had she left it on the bench near Harry's house?

'I took out my sketchbook and pencil,' she thought feverishly, 'and then . . . I put everything down to look at the one they said was Harry . . . I must have left everything on the bench . . .'

Losing the money was terrible, but her sketchbook, her precious drawings . . . She dissolved in tears.

'I've lost everything . . .'

She didn't even feel any pain when she was slapped. She forgot her determination to fight back. She took the blows without a word, gritting her teeth, as she had in the past.

'Go back to where you were,' shouted Aunt Raissa, shaking her by the shoulders. 'You slut, go back to the street or your hotel room! Go on! Get out and don't come back!'

They were still standing in the narrow entrance hall. Ada was leaning against the door. She opened it and ran out. She had so often dreamed of getting away from that house, but without ever having had the courage to face real solitude, poverty and hunger in this strange city. But this scene, after so many others, was more than she could bear. It was better to be out on the street, better to die; she didn't care!

Blinded by tears, she started running, clutching on to the metal handrail along the street. She glanced at the cafés and cheap hotels, terrified, wondering if they would let her spend one night without paying, or whether it would be simpler just to throw herself in front of the next passing car. The party at the Sinners' must be finishing at this very moment, she thought. Why not rush over there and ask for help? She'd already done that once. No! What did she and those people have in common?

Suddenly, she heard someone walking quickly behind her. A hand grabbed her shoulder. She turned around, shaking with fear, still running, out of breath, and then she realised it was Ben. She hated him at that moment as much as she hated Aunt Raissa. She looked at him defiantly and shouted, 'Let go of me! Go away! Leave me alone! I'll never go back, never!'

'Ada! That's enough! Listen to me!'

They stopped. He held her firmly by both arms; she didn't dare fight back because people were watching them from inside the café. But the street was empty.

'Ada! Calm down. Do you want to end up spending the night in prison?'

She suddenly remembered that she was seventeen years old and what was at stake: arrest, reform school. She stood still and silent.

'Ada, don't look at me like that. I've never done you any harm, have I?'

He took her arm and forced her to walk.

'Come on. Let's get out of here. The whole street will be out. Come with me.'

'Where?'

He shrugged his shoulders. 'I don't know. Are you afraid? Don't cry,' he said quickly, squeezing her wrist so hard that she let out a little groan of pain. What could happen to them that was worse?

'I'm not crying,' she whispered.

'Ada, we already found ourselves lost once, all alone like this. Do you remember?'

'Yes, but we knew where to go. We had a home.'

'Any shabby hotel, any hovel or bridge over the Seine would give us more protection than any of the so-called homes we've had up until now. Even when your father was alive, it wasn't a very safe house, sometimes even dangerous, Ada.'

'Leave me alone, Ben, just go away!'

'Do you dislike me as much as you did when we were children, Ada?'

Without replying, she turned a corner. They had no idea where they were going.

'Remember the game?'

'What game?'

'The one you made up . . . Or was it me? Running away in the middle of the night, all alone, while all the grown-ups were fast asleep.'

'Idiot. I was eight.'

'So what?' he said. 'Do people really change?'

'Of course they do.'

'Well, I never stopped dreaming about it. We were alone, abandoned, poor, but there was no one else in sight, not the people you hated, not the ones you loved,' he said finally, more softly.

She stopped, fell on to a bench.

'Ben, what's going to happen to me?'

'Ada, where were you? Who were you with?'

'What do you mean? Are you mad? You believe Aunt Raissa now?'

'Where were you coming from? I'd never seen you like that. Your hair was all dishevelled. You were pale and shaking. You looked as if you had come back from another world,' he said gently.

'I *was* coming back from another world. But I can't talk about it to you, Ben, not even to you . . .'

'Why not?'

'Because you'd laugh at me, and you'd be right . . .'

'Just tell me if you were with another man.'

'A man? Me?'

Her naïve outburst made him smile. He leaned towards her, took her face in his long, rough hands, and with the same cruel yet sensual gesture he'd had since childhood, pinched her cheeks so hard that she cried out.

'Ever since I was thirteen years old,' he then said very softly, 'I've dreamt about you every night . . .'

She pushed him away.

'Are you mad?' she hissed. 'What do you expect from me? I'm not in love with you.'

'Ada, listen to me. You're going to go back home now. Let my mother shout or hit you. Say nothing. As for me, I'll find some work, I'll sort something out, get a little money, and in a few weeks, or a few months, one fine day, we'll just leave, without saying a word to anyone, and we'll get married, Ada.'

'What?'

'We'll get married, do you hear?' he shouted. 'All I need is enough money to pay for a hotel for a few days. That's why I'm asking you to wait.'

'But I'm still a minor.'

He replied in the same quick, passionate tone of voice that had fascinated Ivanov in the past:

'I'll arrange everything. There's always some way or other. Your father isn't legally dead. We can pretend to have his written consent. It's easy. I can fix it. Do you really think anyone will quibble about it? Who cares about us? Oh, if Harry Sinner were getting married you can be sure that everything would be done just the way it should be, properly, according to divine and human laws. But us? Who cares about us?'

'And you really enjoy taking the most tortuous paths, don't you Ben?'

'Tortuous paths? What do you mean?'

'I mean that given a choice between two roads, one of them

clean and bright, the other full of difficulties and secrets, where each step forward is earned by shady, shameful deals, you would never hesitate.'

'And I'll tell you why,' he said, smiling. 'It's because I've never come across those other roads. And again, who would care about us, who would cry over us if things turned out badly? We have no one.'

'It's true that no one would really care about us,' said Ada, sarcastically. 'They'd leave us to starve to death. Have you thought of that?'

'Me? Starve to death? How?' he shouted, teasingly. 'Never, Ada! Never! Starve to death! Other people might. But if you only knew how many secret ways there are to survive – without stealing or killing, don't worry! By trafficking, scheming, buying and selling, always being on the move, by lying!'

'You're just showing off,' she said, shrugging her shoulders. 'You never change, Ben. You think you're stronger and more cunning than everyone else. They'd catch up with you and even on the gallows, you'd still be shouting, "Look at me! I'm better than you!"'

'Idiot,' he said, mocking and bitter, just as when they were children. 'Haven't you ever understood anything? Sure, I show off, I make things up, but when you start out by dreaming of all the things you can't have, you end up getting more than you ever imagined, if you want it badly enough.'

'Do you really think so?' she murmured. 'Really?'

She hid her face in her hands, then shook her head.

'Sometimes I think you're making fun of me and sometimes that you're just mad.'

'We're both a little crazy. We're not logical, we're not philosophers, we're not French, not us! Isn't it just as crazy for a seventeen-year-old to dream of some mysterious man in the same way as when she was eight?'

'Be quiet!'

'I guessed right, then, didn't I?' he said quietly. He'd taken her hand in his and squeezed it hard. 'Well, I'm not laughing, see? So don't you laugh at me. Ada, I swear to you, in six weeks I'll have found enough money to pay for the ring and the first few nights in a hotel. After that, we'll get by. I can't promise you anything else. We'll get by.'

'But I don't need you,' she cried, tears of rebellion in her eyes. 'I can make my own living! I can live by myself. I don't love you. I'd leave you one day.'

'Oh,' he murmured, 'I don't give a damn about the future . . . I can't think past the day when we'll both go out, one at a time, after lunch, me to deliver a package and you to stock up on samples at Printemps department store, the day when we'll come back as husband and wife!'

He burst out laughing. He laughed so loudly, so nervously, that tears streamed down his face.

'Can you picture my mother's face? Can you just see it? She'll kick us both out right away, and by God, we'll go! Don't say that you can live alone, Ada. You're still too young, too sensitive. And I'll let you draw as much as you like.'

He helped her stand up.

'Come on. Is there anything more wonderful than putting up with being treated badly, being humiliated and mocked, while slyly, secretly, planning our revenge? Because my mother will be absolutely furious! Come on, Ada . . . All my life I've been rejected and mocked, but I've kept on thinking, "One day I'll get the better of you. One day, I'll be the strongest."'

'And were you?'

'I am now,' he said, smiling.

Heavy drops of rain began to fall as the storm broke. She followed him home.

A few weeks later, he managed to get some money together

and the documents necessary for their marriage. Everything happened as he had predicted: one day, they each left home to run their separate errands and met at the town hall. They returned to Aunt Raissa's house a married couple. She threw them out. That very evening, they rented a hotel room and began their life as husband and wife.

15

On the Rue des Belles-Feuilles, at the Sinners' home, the tea dance was to finish at eight o'clock.

Harry's mother and aunts called these little parties 'madcap afternoons', the term used to describe them during their youth, in their native city. Whenever they asked: 'Would you do us the honour of coming to our madcap afternoon with your daughter on the Seventeenth?', people found a certain exotic, old-fashioned charm in such an invitation. (Years of living in France had not blotted out their foreign accent, but had refashioned it: they no longer rolled their 'r's the way Russians normally did, but pronounced them more gutturally, which gave a strange Parisian sound to their extremely refined, polite, delightful phrases.) Some even called it 'Slavic charm', in the most well-meaning way.

At eight o'clock, the hum of voices coming from the large green reception room where the buffet was set up grew much softer. Suddenly, fragments of conversation or a particular laugh were clearly audible where, a quarter of an hour earlier, there had merely been the noise of a hundred voices, footsteps and music. But it was only when the tired hostess was able to hear the song of a bird sitting in a tree in the garden (it had stayed on late, fooled by the light) that she allowed herself to hope that she could soon rest. She was standing in the doorway of the scarlet entrance hall, shaking the hand of everyone who was leaving while mechanic-ally reciting the various polite phrases that you shower on guests as you say goodbye, just as a gardener generously offers his flowers every last drop from the watering can.

'But I've hardly had a chance to see you, dear Madame . . . We must arrange to get together . . . Do send your esteemed Mother my very warmest wishes, my dear child . . .' What she was really thinking was: 'It must be nearly nine o'clock.' But she had to make allowances for the latecomers, the perpetually absent-minded, the possessive men who had waited, in vain, for a certain woman to arrive and who refused to give up hope, the couples in love still outside on the stone balcony. She was a good hostess, though, and like most Russians, only happy when the house was bursting with guests. But tonight, she was eager to be alone with Harry, finally to find out.

He had come into the dining room an hour earlier with Laurence Delarcher; the young woman walked a few steps ahead of him and he was looking at her with the passionate concentration that his mother knew so well . . . Ah, from that moment on she had been filled with fear. She could read Harry's face like a book; at least, that was what she believed. Like all mothers, she was simultaneously close, yet far from the truth: things that were staring her in the face went unnoticed, but she had foreseen what even Harry did not yet understand. To her, her son's soul was an ancient parchment on which sometimes only a single word was legible, but that was enough to cast a dazzling light on to the entire scroll. What mother worthy of the name, she thought, would not be the first to recognise that demanding yet humble expression on her son's face that was unique to love as yet unacknowledged? Remembering it, she placed her handkerchief to her heart and, in the light of the setting sun, bluish sparks shot out from the diamonds on her fingers.

'Too many rings . . . She always wears too many rings,' her sisters-in-law would say. But jewellery shouldn't be locked away in the darkness of a safe. Her sisters-in-law had such a boring, masculine way of dressing. Harry's uncles encouraged her to buy jewels: she owed it to herself and to the family name she bore, and it flattered within them a secret, Oriental delight in owning valuable possessions that you could feel in your hands, press to your breast. She shared their way of thinking. Even tonight, it was a consolation to see the dazzling brilliance on her stubby, pale hands. And she needed to be consoled . . . How sad she was tonight. She could sense that Harry and the young woman had spoken to each other of serious matters, said things that would perhaps affect the future. Oh God, her son was still so young! She sighed to herself in Russian: 'God, oh, God!' At times of extreme emotion, she couldn't find the words in French; she suddenly made mistakes when she spoke – she, who had learned French from a Parisian since she was three years old.

'I am so sorry you have to leave at such *a early hour*,' she would say, time and time again, or she would murmur emotionally: 'Where is . . . well, where is *mine* son?'

Her sisters-in-law knew about this weakness and on several occasions had reminded her – acrimoniously – of the famous Jewish story of the wife of a rich banker who is giving birth and whispers in a faint voice: 'My God, I'm in so much pain!' But her husband will only come when she calls him in Yiddish, because when she does that, he knows that it's important and that the child is about to be born. But her sisters-in-law had disagreeable and scathing minds. Besides, they knew no Yiddish, thank God. They hadn't been brought up in the ghetto. Nevertheless, it was undeniable that when upset, it was hard to remember all the rules of French grammar and syntax; they were so difficult.

A few couples still lingered out on the balcony, relishing the coolness of evening. Where was Harry? Was it possible, my

God, that he might be considering marriage? He was only twenty-one.

'Oh my son, my only child,' she moaned to herself, 'I love you so much. Yet marriage is a happy thing. But what do we know? How can we tell? What does God have in store? What will tomorrow bring?' The unconscious, instinctive memory of all the tribulations of the Israelites shot through her mind. She remained standing, in exactly the same spot, automatically reciting her elaborate goodbyes; she looked like all the other women around her, but her magnificent, shiny dark eyes were wild and desperate and she turned her head nervously in all directions, as if she were trying to catch the scent of the wind, wondering from which side disaster would strike. Because if this marriage actually came about ('God forbid!' she thought to herself in Russian, at the same time secretly touching the expensive wood of a table to ward off ill fortune: two lucky charms were better than one, and she had a broad enough mind to borrow superstitions from a variety of cultures), if they really got married, who could predict with certainty that it would make Harry happy? And she wanted to take no chances where he was concerned. She had the extraordinary certainty that some mothers have that he was not destined to be happy. Quite the opposite: she always felt that people were going to harm Harry, hurt him, humiliate him . . . Any marriage carried risks. Any marriage was easy to make, but difficult to protect against danger, like those candles that are lit on the eve of certain holidays, in Russia, on the church porch: despite the snow, despite the wind, they always managed to get the flame to light, but then they had to keep it alight amid gusts of icy wind as they walked home through the dark streets. There were only a few who ever managed it. She herself had been happy in her marriage, even though she now recalled with regret all the moments of jealousy, all the vagaries of conjugal life . . . But most importantly, she and her husband spoke the same language, more or less understood one another, while this young woman, though certainly pretty and from a good family, this young woman was a foreigner. And how was it possible to understand the soul of the French? This girl had such fair hair and rosy cheeks . . . For a moment, Madame Sinner imagined the children who might be born of this union between her son, who had such a dark complexion, and this pretty blonde, and this calmed her. But would the girl's Catholic parents agree to it? She was already suffering in advance, her heart bleeding at the thought of Harry's humiliation if they refused. (Ah, may God preserve and protect us!) 'Why is it that the minute Jews fall in love, love becomes synonymous with fear?' she wondered. She couldn't stand still any longer. She wanted to see him. She made a show of taking one of the ladies by the arm and saying quite loudly, 'No, no, you've only just arrived, I wouldn't hear of you leaving . . . Come and have something to eat . . . some ice cream; it's so hot! Yes, I insist, you can't refuse, come along!'

They walked around the buffet. Harry wasn't there. She dragged her guest towards the balcony. ('It's stifling hot inside, don't you agree?') And there, in the fading light, she saw Harry and Laurence Delarcher, all alone. Everything was silent for a moment.

In an attempt to appear pleasant, she contorted her face into a fixed, sickly smile that made her look like an old street hawker approaching a potential client. Her lined, shrivelled mouth tried in vain to form a Cupid's bow, and her expressive, dark eyes scanned the face and body of the young woman with prodigious speed, 'as though she were trying to judge what I was worth,' thought Laurence.

She wasn't wrong. But his mother wasn't trying to estimate the pennies or francs, just the possibility of happiness, and her heart was breaking with jealousy, concern, aversion and tenderness.

A few moments later, someone came to collect Laurence. Almost everyone had gone by now. You could see the succession of great, airy reception rooms and a fading greenish light that seeped through their open windows; the very last guests wandered past the furniture covered in pale, silver-white satin, looking for their hostess, to say goodbye.

Harry smiled and took his mother's arm: 'Go on, Mama.'

'Harry,' she resisted. 'Harry,' she repeated very quietly, looking at him with the same hopeless, passionate expression she always had when he was ill and she was nursing him, and which was the same whether he had a migraine or pneumonia. 'Harry, my dear, a quick word!'

'Later, Mama, in a minute; we're not alone.'

'Did you ask?' she said, in French, forgetting, as always when she was upset, that in Paris everyone understood the language and that it would have been better to speak a different one if she didn't want people to know what she was saying.

'Yes,' he said.

She crumpled her fine pink handkerchief and pressed it nervously to her lips and nose. She had been extremely well brought up and knew that one mustn't express sadness and disappointment by shouting or swearing, but she was, in spite of everything, from a lower social class than her sisters-in-law, wealthy for only two generations while the Sinners had been wealthy for three. She still had not learned how to display her pain as they could, with trembling lips and a disdainful toss of the head. Her eldest sister-in-law had earned great respect in the family by taking the shock of hearing that her beloved brother had died with a single gesture: she had bowed her head as if in prayer, then raised her eyes to heaven, thus expressing, without uttering a single word, her acceptance of the will of Divine Providence, her sincere distress and her perfect upbringing. Madame Sinner had not attained such heights of refinement: she still found it necessary to wring her bejewelled hands, blink her eyes, groan, sigh, in a word, display in the most spectacular manner the feelings that were oppressing her, feelings that were deep and uncomplicated. She cherished her son. She was afraid for her son.

Harry, meanwhile, looked at her with pity and tender impatience.

'I knew that something bad would happen . . .' she murmured. 'I dreamed of turbid rivers all night long.'

'So you think that my marrying Laurence Delarcher will be a bad thing, Mama?'

Harry knew how to remain impassive, his mouth tightly closed and eyes lowered, but she could see, she could sense, how his sensitive, nervous, delicate body was trembling. Whenever he was scolded as a child (and with such kindness!), she had never heard him complain, but he would tremble afterwards for a long while.

'You're so young, my darling,' she said.

'Well, then, Mama, you'll undoubtedly be pleased to learn that Laurence has turned me down.'

'She turned you down – you? But why?'

He didn't reply. He started to walk away, but she stood in front of him, blocked his path.

'Why did she say no?'

'Her parents would not approve of the marriage,' he explained curtly.

She raised her arms to heaven. Yes, she saw in horror how she must have looked, wringing her hands and raising her arms to heaven. She was beside herself. Her son, her Harry, humiliated, rejected! Her son, unhappy! Each of the sorrows that she felt on his behalf, the pain of seeing him suffer, the fear of losing him – none of these struck a healthy body for the first time; each was a blow to an old wound that had been opened a thousand times, one that endlessly wept and bled.

'We're richer than they are!' she cried with pride.

'Mama,' begged Harry.

'Do you love her, my darling?' she asked, composing herself. 'Do you love her?'

At that moment, she would have gone to the ends of the earth, beseeched the most powerful people in the world (but whom could she implore? And wasn't she, she herself, amongst the most powerful? That idea caused her to feel strangely anxious); she would have allowed herself to be dragged on her knees over sharp stones to secure the very thing she had so dreaded just a few moments before: that young woman marrying her son.

'She'll say yes,' said Harry softly, more to himself than to his worried, trembling mother. 'I'll ask her over and over again,' he thought, 'and I'll wear her down. I'll make myself humble, insistent, imploring.'

Invincible hope had risen from within him, hope born of defeat, aroused and nourished by that very defeat.

His mother was still talking; he didn't reply, but gently left her side and went to join one of the guests who was saying goodbye to his aunts. A little while later, the last car left. Harry went up to his room. The first drops of rain from the storm suddenly began falling over Paris.

16

The established Delarcher French Bank was on good terms with the international bank owned by the Sinners, but to go from there to thinking that a marriage between Laurence and the young Sinner might be desirable, even possible – no! These foreigners who came from goodness knows where were so arrogant: you offered them hospitality and they marched into your house like conquerors, thought Laurence's father. He pretended not to notice his daughter's red eyes. He was outraged and annoyed. In love? Nonsense! At eighteen! He could still picture her in a little dress and short socks running into the dining room, in the countryside, on summer mornings (she wore a little pinafore with flowers on it) . . . And now, love, marriage. Of course he would see her married. But later on . . . He glanced at her furtively with anger and dismay. He loved her the way a busy father does: he was brusque, masculine, undemonstrative, unemotional, and expressed any affection in an impatient voice and hurried gestures. Whenever one of his four children came to ask him for something, Delarcher would snap at them in sullen, preoccupied tones: 'Fine! So? What of it?' And with a quick wave of the hand, he seemed immediately to sweep away, brush aside, all their arguments and logic. Then he would continue, more loudly: 'Well, *I'm* telling you . . .'

or 'This is what you're going to do.' The three eldest children were of an age when you start to become worn down by life: the two girls were married; the boy was twenty-five; they had become more docile, more malleable than when they were very young, but what could be done with an eighteen-year-old? The age when you attack obstacles with the foolish stubbornness of a buzzing bee banging against a closed window? Was it possible that Laurence might really be in love? The very thought of her and that little Sinner loving each other made the blood rush to his enormous head and right through his grey hair. He waved his knife and fork about in rage. Laurence would tell him nothing . . . She was shy with him, secretive, and he preferred it that way. For a young girl to talk of love was . . . dangerous, pointless, in any case. He was a French father, with a great sense of propriety. A marriage arranged by him, with all the details of the contract and the dowry discussed by the family, made marriage itself less offensive. It embellished or even hid anything that had to do with the physical side of a union. But love! A young girl in love, well, really!

And yet, he was moved. He had often felt this complicated mixture of irritation and uneasiness where his children were concerned. When they were ill, or when he had to punish them, he felt a mixture of pity, anger and almost a vague disgust. He had a sharp, quick mind and he greatly valued that quality in himself, but it was to all intents and purposes worthless when it came to his relationships with women and children: those irrational creatures he couldn't prevent himself from thinking of as inferior. They lived in a shadowy world that he approached with the greatest mistrust, the greatest fear. Approached? No! He preferred to avoid it, to look away, to remain silent, as he did now. No one knew how to hide his most secret thoughts better than this passionate, eloquent man if he believed it the wisest thing to do . . . And besides, life ends up teaching us that it is impossible to help other people, in spite of good will, in spite of love . . . No, we can do nothing for others, not when they suffer, not when they are ill, not when they are dying. He had felt this most powerfully for the first time when his wife had suffered for forty-eight hours when bringing Laurence into the world. From that day onwards, he had worked out a specific philosophy that applied to anything that affected his family, a way of thinking comprised of authority and flexibility in equal parts. It was necessary to shape children's lives, lead them by force, if necessary, on to the path you believed was best for them, but you could not suffer for them; you had to allow them to solve their problems by themselves. Firmly hold the hand of the child at the edge of the river when he wants to jump in to pick some beautiful flower. Respect the child's sadness at not being able to have what he wants. Be authoritarian and even tyrannical where actions are concerned, but avoid the desire to look deep into the souls of those in your care.

No, such a marriage was not desirable. Not that Laurence's father was a believer . . . Besides, it was not simply a question of his being Jewish; he was a foreigner. One does not marry, one does not allow a foreigner into the family. No, that was surely too quick and haughty a judgment. The truth was that, in his mind, there was a distinction between various categories of foreigners. An Anglo-Saxon or someone from the Mediterranean was still acceptable . . . One of his sisters had married a Spaniard. It was impossible to comment on the union for the poor woman had died in childbirth. Yet he couldn't help but think that a Frenchman would have known how to give his wife children without exposing her to death. But he had remained on good terms with his brother-in-law. He wasn't actually xenophobic, no . . . yet everything that came from the East aroused insurmountable mistrust within him. Slavonic, Levantine, Jewish – he didn't know which of these terms disgusted him the most. There was nothing you could count on, nothing solid . . . Take the Sinners' fortune, for example. It was a great fortune, certainly. Too great, no doubt, precarious, unstable . . . There were those sugar refineries in the Ukraine and Poland: the original ones had been sold before the Russian Revolution, or so people said; the new ones were working at full capacity . . . Really? It was all so vague, changeable, incomprehensible . . . A fortune abroad, foreign dealings . . . Oh, it was bad, all that, bad . . . The bank itself belonged to Harry's uncles; Harry was completing an apprenticeship until the day he would join as a partner. The bank was famous throughout the world. It irritated him because of its international connections, its reputation, its legendary secret power. A solid family business, as sound as his, linked by marriage to a bank owned by foreigners? No. His own company had grown from an established bank in the provinces, run by his family from generation to generation. As for the Sinners' . . . establishment, that surely had its roots in some money-lender's shop, some second-hand stall, some small-time usurer. Ah, how distasteful he would find such a marriage!

His hostility was perhaps based on physical impressions. Harry's uncles were short men, with greasy skin, sharp features, anxious eyes. Delarcher was a giant with a very ruddy face, thick eyebrows and a booming voice. He had often dined at the Sinners' house and he felt deeply condescending towards those miserable people who complained about their upset stomachs, kept to a diet and would only allow themselves 'the tiniest bit of Rhine wine' at the end of a meal. German wine? In France? The land of Burgundies and champagne! It was an insult. And the way they moved, as silently and stealthily as a cat. And they looked so alike! They were twins. You never knew if you were talking to Salomon or Isaac. They would suddenly appear at your side, with that little ironic, anguished smile so unique to their race. He disliked everything about the Sinners' house. Luxurious, but in bad taste. Unbelievable waste! And those women . . . Oh my God, the mother, that fat Jewess covered in jewellery! And the aunts, coy, affected, reading Nietzsche . . . What a family! Slavs, Germans,

Jews, they were as bad as each other. The same guardedness, the same sense of mistrust. Ambiguous, incomprehensible . . . And he disliked the boy. That was the most serious thing. First of all, he didn't like his looks: he was delicate, nervous, short. And his hair . . . You could tell, thought Delarcher with his thick grey hair, you could tell that the boy had to do everything in his power to straighten his hair every morning just to hide his natural curls. His eyes shone with a bright, passionate expression, as if they were burning in hot oil. And his pale, yellowish complexion . . . He was young, but his skin showed no signs of youth or freshness.

'He looks old,' thought Delarcher, scornfully. 'Was it possible that Laurence really cared for him? Women are a mystery.'

Meanwhile, the Delarchers' excellent dinner, comprised of numerous courses, was coming to an end. Laurence's brother and her older sisters were chatting loudly, trying to cheer up their father, who was clearly in a bad mood. Only Laurence said nothing. While they were having dessert, her father suddenly turned to her and said sharply, 'If you're tired, go upstairs and go to bed. There's nothing more foolish than coming down to dinner with a cold like you have. And your eyes are all swollen,' he said, shrugging his shoulders and turning to look at the rest of the family. 'Go on, off you go!'

It was all he could do for her: allow her to be alone, to shed some tears into her pillow. She got up and went over to him to give him a kiss.

'You'll feel better tomorrow, right?' he asked quietly, with the impatient, mocking tone of voice she knew so well, and that she liked because, to her, it was the personification of masculine strength.

She leaned down so he could kiss her cheek, then looked at him and said, 'I don't know.'

It was only then that Delarcher began to feel afraid.

17

Two years later, Harry was waiting for Laurence at the corner of the street where she lived. Laurence would come out alone; no one suspected their meetings, which, although innocent, filled her with remorse. Each guilty step she took was hampered by an innate hesitation which meant she was unable to enjoy anything that was not strictly permissible. As a child, she had never taken delight in being disobedient. She could only live and breathe in a world where everything was precise, clear and well defined, with no grey areas and no guilty pleasures. In spite of that, she agreed to keep seeing Harry. She loved him.

For a long time, she had feared this love. It was not in her nature to allow her heart to be filled by an emotion that was so overwhelming and so passionate without mistrusting it. The excessive, romantic, dramatic side of such passion, which she would smile and call 'like the Capulets and Montagues', seemed to her, if not actually ridiculous, at least strange. And, like her father, she disliked anything that seemed, at first glance, strange, foreign. No, she didn't welcome this love, the way Ada would have done, as the dried-up land soaks in the rain, but rather with insight, discernment and reserve: just as certain beautiful roses in the gardens of France can be drenched by a storm and still not lose a single leaf or petal. The driving rain covers them in huge drops that only penetrate them gradually, gently, until they reach the rose's heart. In his mind, Harry had often compared Laurence to those fresh, hardy roses, their petals tightly furled. It had not been easy working his way into her secretly rebellious heart, but he had accomplished it now, and he reigned there. It was his reward for his long fidelity, his passionate love. He loved her so much. He walked beside her down the empty street (it was barely nine o'clock in the morning, there was no danger of being seen; she was going to classes), and the expression on his face was so tortured, so strange that Laurence murmured:

'Don't look at me like that.'

'Why not? There's not a soul in sight.'

'You sometimes look at me in a way that makes me feel ashamed.'

He knew that her modesty was not feigned. He also knew that it was not coldness, but rather the sign of a passion so burning and alive that she feared its force. He took her hand and squeezed it, sliding his fingers between her glove and bare skin.

'Harry,' she said, pulling away, 'I've spoken to my father again.'

He stopped, turning pale. Never had she seen a human face express so many nuances of sadness, from fear to wounded pride, yet he possessed neither words nor gestures when it came to joy. She felt sorry for him; she wanted to see him radiant, childlike, if possible, but his serious, tortured face always made him look older than he was. He stood anxious and incredulous as she spoke:

'He's given his consent, Harry.'

A second later, flames suddenly rose to his pale cheeks, as if he finally understood, as if the words had seeped right down to his heart, extinguishing within him an unquenchable anguish.

'This is a great victory,' he said very quietly.

If he suffered more than others, he also knew how to enjoy his triumphs better. Only the strange joy of a conscious, fierce exhilaration was able to wipe away all those years of unhappiness. For he had been very unhappy because of her, because of his secret, scorned love ... Now, at last, she was accepting him, she loved him. He would have happily died for her.

'Is it true? How did it happen? What did he say?'

She didn't reply. She couldn't repeat what he'd said. She and her parents had fought continuously for two years. Her father had been the first to be worn down. She had wished for that moment for so long, and now, she almost regretted it because it was poisoned by pity and remorse. She had never noticed how her father had aged in those two years, but, last night, when he had said, still shaking with anger, 'Very well! On your head be it, but don't come looking to me, don't come complaining to me later on', it was only then that she had seen his deep wrinkles, his sagging jaw, the thinness of his neck where his Adam's apple jutted out, as if up until that moment her love had blinded her in the most literal sense of the word. And Harry, how triumphant he looked now! A victory, he'd called it. She could feel her father's defeat right down to her very core.

But could she tell Harry what he had said? All the pointless, unfair, harsh words ... Harry seemed to guess. The joyful expression on his face disappeared.

'I can imagine what he must have said,' he replied bitterly.

He fell silent, while there, in the darkness of the car they had got into, with tenderness, pity and a strange feeling of resentment, she kissed him for the very first time.

18

One day, a stranger was introduced to Lilla. 'He's a Kurd or a Hindu,' said her colleague, one of the other women who, like her, performed naked in the Music Hall, 'but he looks rather shabby.'

He fell in love with Lilla and began sending her chocolates and flowers. He looked poor, with threadbare clothes, which made Lilla feel sorry for him, and since she did not attach an exaggerated sense of importance to the gift of her body, one day she chided him affectionately, 'You're mad to make such a drama out of something so simple. Do you want to sleep with me? Just say it: "I want to sleep with you." What's the point of sending chocolates and flowers? Life is hard for everyone. You'll end up with no money at all.'

The man reacted in an extraordinary way to her frank words.

'Are you saying you don't know who I am?' he asked, his voice choking.

She had no idea. He told her his family name. He was part of a minor eastern monarchy who ruled a land that provided oil to England; for this reason, the civil list of the royal family was paid in pounds sterling. Never, he told her, had he met such an unselfish woman. It was her Slavic character, he said, kissing her hands, her goodness that had charmed him, and since she was, on the other hand, very pretty . . . would she? Lilla felt dizzy, already picturing herself the wife of a king and the mother of princes. Unfortunately, he was married. He did, however, offer her an enviable future: a palace where central heating had just been installed in the capital city of his country, an apartment in Paris and a new wardrobe. He was leaving the next day; she must come too.

Lilla tried to think of someone other than Aunt Raissa to whom she could tell her good luck; she remembered her young sister-in-law Ada and rushed over to her house. They saw each other occasionally. Once faced with the *fait accompli*, Aunt Raissa had given in: she couldn't help but feel secret admiration for anyone who stood up to her. It was a strange fact to Ada that their poor lodgings in the Ternes district now seemed rather welcoming and pleasant. After all, she had no other home. She had worked very hard at the beginning of her marriage: she had been a dressmaker, a salesgirl, a secretary. For a few months now, Ben had been earning some money, so she could paint again. She was twenty years old, with brusque gestures and a pale, expressive face. When she was interested in something, fire rushed to her thin cheeks, turning them a deep red, but normally her paleness made her skin look yellowish and sickly, especially since she hated make-up and never knew how to put it on properly. She was petite, with a good figure, though she was still too thin. Marriage had barely filled her out: she had remained lanky, like a young girl, and her gestures were rapid and passionate, as in the past. She now wore her hair pulled back, but when she was working, it fell forward over her eyebrows in a thick, dark fringe, just as it had when she was a child. Her young forehead bore the mark of a painter: the deep vertical wrinkle between the eyebrows that comes from the effort of concentrating, focusing, passionately staring at whatever is being studied and recreated. The room in which Ada lived with Ben was humble, but clean and very light. When Lilla came in, Ada was drawing the portrait of a young Jewish woman from the Rue des Rosiers, a female face with skin like wax, dark eyes that were warm, sly, brilliant; she already had a double chin and a fake pearl necklace and her glossy hair fell on to her cheek in a kiss-curl. She was a Lithuanian immigrant, one of Ada's neighbours who sometimes posed for her.

Lilla didn't even wait for her to leave before beginning to tell what had happened in a breathless voice.

'Silly little goose,' thought Ada. Her cousin seemed destined for such love affairs; she passively accepted whatever life offered her – caresses or slaps on the face. Because of her foolishness, she avoided the curse of a race that was unable to find peace, but which endlessly, vainly, sought to be stronger than God Himself. Ada found Lilla refreshing.

'I won't forget about you, Ada. I'll help you. I'll send you money.'

Ada smiled and thanked her. She knew very well that as soon as Lilla left the country, she'd forget everything. It wasn't a flaw in her character, rather her good fortune . . . the little birdbrain . . . How little the brother and sister resembled each other, she thought.

'How are you getting by?'

'Not badly,' Ada replied. 'Of course, we're not happy in a way the French would understand.'

The people in their building were deeply wary of Ben and Ada: they were young, and didn't seem to know what a hot meal was, or a stew, or a slow-cooked soup; they spoke a foreign language and walked quickly past you, eyes lowered, as if they were afraid of you . . . Ah, they were foreigners . . . That was it; that summed it up. Wanderers with no roots, immigrants, suspicious. On the whole, people instinctively hated Ben and felt sorry for Ada. But even then, there was a depth of incomprehension that couldn't be overcome by any amount of good will on the part of compassionate neighbours who thought, 'Poor little thing, alone all day long,' and Ada, who secretly led her life in a virtual dream-world, beyond the bounds of reality. And as far as comforts were concerned – little meals affectionately prepared, hats decorated with a metre of ribbon bought in a sale, pleasant evenings spent in the soft light of a lamp beside a husband who read the papers in his slippers while a child slept on his lap – as far as the French way of life was concerned, so beautiful, so harmonious, so envi-able . . . it was . . . it should have been attractive, but it was as challenging and foreign to Ben and Ada as a sedentary lifestyle on fertile plains would have seemed to nomads.

'Oh Ada, you've always lived life as if you were sleepwalking,' Lilla said mockingly.

She suddenly went over to her cousin and gave her a kiss.

'Ada, Adotchka, forgive me, I'm an idiot, I'm completely mad. I swear that I will never forget you, but you never know, you never know . . . So, while I'm here, I want to give you a present. Listen, I have ten thousand francs in my handbag. Yes, he just gave me the money to buy some clothes and a suitcase for the trip. Let's share it. But you have to promise that it's just for you, so you can get something you really want, and not for Ben.'

'Why not for Ben?'

'He'll manage without either of us. I've never met anyone like Ben. I'm positive that even water couldn't drown him or fire burn him.'

'But he'll find the money you give me, really!'

'So hide it, you little fool!'

Ada took the five thousand francs Lilla gave her. When her cousin left, the first thing she did was go and look over the work she had done that day. With her perceptive eye, she studied the voluptuous, fleshy face, the hooked nose, the fake pearls and satin dress, threadbare at the elbows, which she had painted on the canvas. Some of it was good: there, and there . . . the yellowish glint, like the colour of some ancient candle, contrasted with her mouth, covered in geranium red lipstick, and the misty expression that seeped out from beneath her heavy eyelids. But the satin wasn't the dazzling bright blue it should have been. She hesitated for a long time, palette in hand, then threw it down. She found the portrait simultaneously attractive and unpleasant. Why didn't she paint elegant young women, in beautiful gardens, delicate hats, fountains, June flowers? She couldn't. It wasn't her fault. She was driven to seek out, cruelly, tirelessly, the secrets concealed in sad faces, beneath dark skies. She pressed her forehead against the window, then took the money Lilla had given her and went out.

She started walking towards Harry's house. Since she had got married and was free to go where she pleased, she had often gone back to stand beneath those windows, mocking herself, but finding humble, passionate, exquisite pleasure in such a pointless act. It was not only the darkness, the presence of Harry that she now sought. It was the brief flashes of a more beautiful life, one that was sweeter and, most especially, less brutal than her own, for she sensed there was something abnormal about her existence. More than once, she had run into Harry with Laurence. She had followed them, listening to them, watching them, imagining what being in love might mean to them. She had guessed they were engaged. She thought that a young Frenchwoman wouldn't go out that way, alone with a man, unless she was promised to him. Sometimes she only caught a glimpse of them for a moment before they hurried into Harry's car. But at other times, they would walk the few steps to the corner of the street where there was a shop that sold antiquarian books. They would go into the shop. Ada could see them, through the window: Harry would pick up the beautiful books and run his hands over them; she felt genuine fascination as she watched his dark, agile hands softly stroking their tawny or red covers. One day, a few weeks earlier, Ada had seen them bargaining over a rare book that they didn't buy, and when they'd come out of the shop, she'd heard Laurence say, 'I'm telling you, it's madness . . .'

How sensible she was, Ada thought. How wonderful to be like this foreign young woman, to be able to choose dresses, furniture for the drawing room, a governess for the children, beautiful linen for the dining table with such ease. Ada imagined her buying her wedding trousseau, feeling the sheets to judge the quality of the fabric. Yet today, she, Ada, had the power to fulfil one of Harry's desires. More than once, she had stared at that book, so coveted by him. It occupied the place of honour in the shop; it cost . . . almost all the money that Lilla had given her. Ada went into the bookshop; she asked to see the book. She looked at it curiously. So this is what he had wanted; he might even have forgotten about it by now . . . But she would give it to him. She had never given a present to anyone, except Lilla and Madame Mimi when she could – trinkets that cost a few pennies or a little bouquet of flowers. It had given her so much pleasure . . . As for buying a present for Ben, he liked neither beautiful clothes, nor fine food, nor rare books. There was something spartan about Ben. The idea of offering him a gift seemed as strange as tying a ribbon around the neck of a wolf. But Harry . . . She smiled, her eyes sparkled. She knew what she was doing only too well: she felt a strange mixture of madness and cunning rise within her. Harry was courting, in love with this foreign young woman. He doubtlessly thought only of her, he was obsessed by her, and now she, Ada, was going to insinuate herself between them. He would be intrigued by this gift (naturally, she would leave the book for him at his house with no note). He would go and question the book-seller. He would never guess the truth. But he wouldn't be able to stop himself from thinking about Ada, without knowing who she was, just as she had dreamt of him, in vain, for such a very long time. She would steal a dream, a sigh, a wish from him. She could ask for nothing more.

She walked to Harry's house. She handed the book to the servant who answered the door. She was so violently overcome with emotion that she couldn't say a single word: she knew her voice would shake. She simply pointed to the address she had written on the back of the package in pencil.

'Do you want a receipt?' the servant asked.

She forced herself to speak:

'No, no receipt,' she said in a steady voice.

All she could do was whisper the words, lowering her eyes, quivering.

The servant looked at her in surprise and closed the door. Ada thrust her bare hands deep into the pockets of her jacket and, suddenly overcome with panic, ran down the steps. She only stopped running when she got to the next street, far from Harry's house, where she felt safe.

Now she mocked and berated herself fiercely. She was mad. She, a woman of twenty, had behaved like a little twelve-year-old child. 'But I'm not a woman,' she thought. 'There are people who are ageless, and I'm one of them. I was an old woman at twelve, and even when I have white hair I'll be exactly the same in my heart as I am today. Why be ashamed of it?'

That young girl, that French woman whom he loved, how she would have laughed if she'd known! Suddenly, a desperate prayer rose from the depths of Ada's soul:

'Why, my God, why didn't you make him mine? He was made for me, meant for me, and I for him . . . Make him mine! I'll put up with anything: being abandoned when he grows tired of me, the pain, the shame, anything in the world, but just make him mine! It isn't possible that I could have loved him for so long, in vain, if it were not Your will to bring us together one day. Make him mine, Lord . . .'

The street was dark, deserted. No one could see that she was crying.

19

Harry and Laurence had been married for more than three years when, one day, on his way to visit his mother, Harry stopped in front of the bookshop at the corner of the street. He noticed two small paintings on display amongst the rare books. They were both landscapes. In one, a sloping street lined with a few low houses was covered in melting snow, while a reddish light the colour of rubies (a smoking lamp lit behind a window) illuminated the strange, desolate dusk that looked as if it were made of ashes, ochre and iron. The second painting was a garden, partly wild, on a spring day; the fresh, young grass, the flowers and the blue sky all had an extraordinary luxuriance, warmth and richness that did not exist in this country, but which seemed familiar to Harry, something he recognised from deep within his memory. Surely, thought Harry, struck by a strong, confusing impression, surely he had seen this somewhere before, in a dream or during his childhood: those dark March skies where gusts of snow fell, and those wild gardens, teeming with the flowers of a short, stiflingly hot summer.

He shaded his eyes with his hand, as if to shelter them from the too brilliant light, for the memory (if it really was a memory and not a dream), the memory aroused both joy and sadness, he didn't know why . . . It was like the way certain faces, certain unfamiliar houses awaken a trace of something in the mind that is at once melancholy yet sweet, as if witness to some past life. No, it wasn't a dream, but a distant reality, one destroyed very long ago . . . He could picture them again now, those March days, in the country where he'd been born, when snowstorms raged in the town. In spite of the storms, the first hyacinths began to bloom, protected behind thick windows, announcing the arrival of spring. He felt as if he could once again smell their perfume, a scent linked in his mind to the smell of birthday cake. His birthday was in March. On that day, almost every year throughout his childhood, he had been ill, or at least the people around him thought he was ill. He would cough, and that certainly meant he might be getting whooping cough; or he had slept badly and might have a fever. It was safer for him to stay in his bedroom; and so, locked in a hot room, with toys he didn't touch, he sadly contemplated the diagonal pattern of the snowflakes as they fell. How strange it was . . . He recalled the rich and somewhat sickly smell of the enormous chocolate cakes on which his name, Harry, was written in pink icing. The light of that soft, grey sky summoned up a whole string of people, hardly recognisable, forgotten: servants, pets, teachers, his grandfather with his hawk-like nose and piercing eyes, his petite, shy grandmother who had never got used to the luxury of the house. He could picture her now, sitting at the very edge of the gilded chairs, holding Harry close and stroking her grandson's hair while tenderly murmuring words in a foreign language. She alone still spoke Yiddish, which the others found scandalous.

He turned to look at the second painting. The hot summer days, the tinkling bell of the ice cream seller, the flowers crushed under foot, crumpled in people's hands, too many plants, too many flowers, a perfume that was overly sweet, that troubled and lulled the spirit; too much light, a savage glare, the songs of birds in the sky: this was his land, his past, and he was rediscovering it.

He had walked into the bookshop without thinking, but overcome by inexplicable shyness, he didn't yet ask to see the paintings; he picked up books at random, felt them, opened them.

'Are you selling paintings now?' he asked at last.

'No, Monsieur Harry,' replied the bookseller, who had known him since he was a schoolboy and helped him put together the valuable library that he had begun creating aged fifteen. 'No, but the artist, who is young and unknown, asked me to display them, as a favour. She's a woman,' he added after a moment of silence.

'Ah!' said Harry.

But whether the painter was a man or a woman didn't concern him.

'I'd quite like to see them,' he said.

He took them and leaned them against a stack of books. He became engrossed in studying the sombre sky, the small hovels that seemed whipped by the wind. He felt intense, exquisite pleasure when he looked at the golden, fiery garden. The northern springtime when icy fog and windy storms gave way to an intoxicating, wondrous summer... how could he have forgotten it all?

'They're not bad,' he said out loud, forcing himself to sound indifferent.

'Not bad at all, especially when you think they're the work of a young woman who can't be more than twenty. But then, I think you know her, don't you?'

'Me? No.'

'Didn't you see her name?'

He hadn't thought to look. He made it out in the corner of the painting: 'Ada Sinner'.

'Well, that's funny,' he said, recognising his own name. 'A young girl of twenty, you say? What does she look like?'

The bookseller smiled.

'You really don't know who she is?'

'No. Why?'

'Because . . . Do you remember that book that was mysteriously sent to you a few years ago, just before you got married? It was the same young woman who bought it.'

'That isn't possible!' cried Harry, with a sharp gesture of surprise.

'I recognised her at once. She has dark brown hair, rather beautiful; she looks foreign.'

'Have you had these paintings here for long?'

'Several months. You've walked past them twenty times without ever looking at them. I think the young woman only insisted I take them because she hoped that one day, sooner or later, you'd notice them. That was partly why I agreed, and also because she was so determined . . . I've never met anyone more persuasive. In the end, it was impossible not to give in.'

Harry frowned. He had more or less guessed the truth. He didn't associate Ada with the little girl who had appeared at his house on the day of a pogrom, in the wind and snow, but he sensed that she was a compatriot and a Jew, undoubtedly all alone in Paris and clinging to the name of the rich Sinners as to a supreme hope. Like all Jews, he was more sharply, more sadly scandalised than a Christian by the faults that were specifically Jewish. And that tenacious energy, that almost savage need to get what one wants, that blind scorn for whatever anyone else might think, all these things were classed in his mind in a single category: 'Jewish arrogance'.

He had absolutely no desire whatsoever to meet this Ada Sinner.

'I'll gladly buy these two paintings,' he said to the bookseller, 'but you must handle all the negotiations and you can't say that I am the buyer. This young woman must be some distant relation and I haven't the slightest inclination to meet her. But I like the paintings. Ask her how much she wants.'

20

Harry had no desire to meet Ada Sinner but he couldn't stop himself from talking about her paintings and showing them to guests who came to see him. People liked them; they found them realistic yet poetic in a strange, wild way. At the lunches that Laurence gave, there was always a small group of people asking where 'the pictures by the unknown artist' were. Harry kept them in his own room; it was elegant, with a bay window that shed an unusually soft light on the two paintings.

And so Ada's name began to become known in a social circle whose very existence was as obscure to her as some faraway planet, while she continued living her poor, lonely life. One day, some friends of Harry and Laurence who had lunched with them remarked that, after all, this young woman might have other works to show them, just as interesting as these. They proposed to go and visit her in her studio, if she was still alive and well, and living in Paris. It would be amusing, they thought, to turn up at her door with no warning, to dangle before her eyes the possibility of fame and fortune, ready to forget her in an instant, however, if she did not completely live up to the hopes they placed in her. Naturally, they didn't put it in this way: they were full of good intentions, they were civilised and caring, but curious and always eager for new experiences. After all, they loved Art above all else. Hadn't one of them even said – she was an American with rosy cheeks and white hair – 'I simply couldn't live without music. I would even abandon my sick child to get to Salzburg to hear *Eine kleine Nachtmusik*.' But she said anything that came into her mind without thinking. She had no way of knowing what she would really do at the bedside of a sick child: she only had dogs.

Harry – he didn't know why – tried to dissuade them; but they were so enthusiastic, like children eager to see some new spectacle, that they finally convinced their host.

'Oh really, Harry! You know you're mad about this young woman's painting!'

'It's not that. I think she has both talent and awkwardness in equal parts, but she also has a wild, dark side . . .'

'Exactly, and you adore that . . .'

He said nothing. How could he make them understand the superstitious thrill that gripped him whenever he looked at those paintings? It was like stepping into an abandoned house where people you once knew and loved had lived, but were now dead. What was the point of saying anything? It was better to give in.

'It will be my pleasure to go with you, if you like,' he replied politely.

The men, their faces red after the long meal and the excellent old wines that Laurence served, and the women, who'd touched up their make-up, left, heading for Ada's lodgings, whose address they had obtained from the bookshop on the Rue des Belles-Feuilles.

They walked up the stark staircase. Ada came and opened the door when they rang. She seemed extremely young, almost a child, they thought. The short skirt she wore added even more to the impression of extreme youth. Her dress was several years old, when they were made very short, above the knee. As soon as Ada saw the strangers, she thought of her inappropriate skirt and blushed; tears welled up in her eyes. She looked unhappy, terrified and defiant. She took a few steps back. Harry caught the look she gave them from beneath her long eyelashes, a quick, piercing look, rapidly suppressed, that seemed to beg the familiar walls for help.

'Poor little thing,' thought Harry.

He wanted to reassure her.

'Forgive us for intruding on you in your studio,' he said softly, 'but I and the people here are great admirers of the two little paintings of yours that I recently acquired. We wanted to tell you that.'

She thanked them. Her voice shook at first, but she ended her brief sentence rather calmly. Laurence, who had been moved by the obvious emotion of the young woman, felt suddenly colder towards her, even hostile. These foreigners had such confidence . . . all hidden beneath a ridiculous shyness. This young woman already seemed so at ease. Only Harry noticed how she quickly put her hands behind her back, presumably so that no one could see they were shaking.

'Come in,' she said, nodding towards the door.

She blushed again sadly when she caught them staring at the shabby furniture. They gathered around her easel. Feelings of curiosity, excellent intentions, the desire to shine, to be amused, to have their spirits soar, rushed through them, drove them towards Ada, inspired exclamations of admiration, as if they were at a zoo, studying a rare, wild animal in its cage.

'But how old are you?'

'Twenty-three.'

'So young! How could you possibly paint like this?'

'I work a lot,' Ada replied.

But her explanation was too simple to satisfy the need for the miraculous that lives in every person's heart.

'No!' they immediately cried out. 'What you do is so sincere, ingenuous, barbaric! That's what's so beautiful!'

'Don't you find there's something Dostoyevskian about her?' a woman murmured, looking Ada up and down through her lorgnette.

'Are you related to Harry?'

Ada and Harry looked at each other and smiled. She broke through the circle that surrounded him, walked towards the young man and asked quietly, 'You are my cousin, Harry Sinner, aren't you?'

'Yes. I've seen you before; I remember now, but it's as distant as a dream.'

'You don't remember Israel Sinner, who worked for your grandfather a long time ago, back home?'

'I don't recall.'

'And you don't remember a little boy and girl who hid in your house one morning? The morning of a pogrom?' she asked, looking sharply around her and lowering her voice even more, just as someone who knows a secret rite speaks more softly in a crowd when only one person is meant to understand.

'I remember now,' said Harry.

And his face, normally so cold and impassive, suddenly became so passionate, so attentive, so like the boy he once was, that Ada lost all her shyness.

'Really? You really remember?'

'Yes: a little boy with torn clothes and a little girl with wonderful eyes, a long fringe and a thick head of black, dishevelled hair ... How could I have not recognised you? That is one of the most vivid memories of my childhood in a way, one of the clearest, one that is cutting through me again right now, one that I still dream of. Yes,' he whispered, looking at Ada in surprise, 'I dream about you, very often.'

She pictured him so clearly, beside his sleeping wife, in his large

French bed, dreaming about her, that an extraordinary feeling of joy filled her heart.

He smiled.

'But my dream always ends up as a nightmare. You come in, take me by the hand and lead me God knows where . . .'

He laughed, but with a slight quiver of pain on his lips. 'You aren't angry?' he asked.

'No. But even in a dream, I could never hurt you.'

'That little boy, what happened to him?'

'I married him.'

'He was ugly . . . but he also had a face that you don't forget.'

'Do you remember,' Ada suddenly asked, 'the weather, the air back home? The evenings on the riverbank? The streets near where you lived had so many lime trees that, in springtime, you walked beneath an archway of blossom and on a carpet of flowers. And the dust in summer?'

'The shouts of the *chouroum-bouroum*, the carpet seller,' murmured Harry.

'A Tartar who went from door to door?'

'Yes. And the little red-headed children, the acrobats who came to perform outside people's windows in winter?'

'And the crazy old man who had sung at the Opera and thought he was still a singer, draping himself with faded fine clothing, a crown of dried leaves on his head, making grand gestures and imagining that he was singing, though not a sound escaped his lips?'

'Yes. And the snow fell on him and his beard was tossed about in the wind; and when the children were naughty, the maid would threaten them: "Be quiet or I'll give you to the crazy old singer."'

'Why did you send me a gift a few years ago?' he asked suddenly, with no affectation or harshness, but with a strange kind of anguish. 'Why do something so mad?'

'I don't know. I had to.'

'So mad!' he said once more.

This time, she remained calm. She looked at him pensively, sadly.

'You can't imagine what you've meant to me.'

'But that was . . . back home . . . so long ago . . .'

'Yes, back home . . . but what happened there is perhaps more important than you might think, more important than anything else, even your life here, your marriage. We were born there; our roots are there . . .'

'You mean in Russia?'

'No. Before that . . . further back than that . . .'

'It isn't just some climate or particular place on earth,' murmured Harry, 'but a specific way of loving, of desiring . . .'

'What have you desired most in the world?'

'The young woman I married. And you?'

'To know you.'

'If you desired it as passionately, as hopelessly, as I desired . . . having Laurence,' he said very quietly, 'well, then, I feel sorry for you.'

'Hopelessly? Why do you say that? You have her.'

'Yes,' he said, somewhat bitterly. 'Like an object seen in a mirror, a reflection, a shadow, but which you can neither grasp hold of, nor . . .'

He stopped.

'Don't listen to me. I demand the impossible. The truth is, I'm happy.'

People were walking towards them.

'I want to help you; I want to see you again . . .' he said hurriedly. 'What can I do to help you?'

'Nothing, oh nothing,' said Ada quickly. 'I'm happy that you have the two little paintings in your house.'

'Can't I do anything for that boy . . . your husband?'

She shook her head.

'No, nothing.'

People were coming towards them. She walked away from him without saying a word.

21

When Harry and his wife got home, Laurence immediately went in to see the baby, who was twenty months old; carrying him in her arms, she returned to where Harry was waiting for her. It was an hour before dinner and the child's bedtime. One by one, all the rituals were carried out: Harry watched his son roll about on the carpet; he sang him a song, walked around with him perched on his shoulders, pretended to box with him, and finally, when he was excited, happy, his cheeks red, his black curls having lost their beautifully controlled shape and turned back into the frizzy, dishevelled mass God had intended, he handed him over to his Swiss governess.

He went back into the library. Laurence placed a small table next to his armchair that held his ashtray, the book he was reading and a glass of sherry, then she switched on the lamp. Each of her gestures was graceful, Harry thought once more. No one could arrange flowers, light a fire, adjust a lampshade better than her. At the beginning of their marriage, Harry thought he would never tire of watching her coming and going, doing the simplest of things. During their secret engagement, this was what he most often, most happily imagined: walking beside her, sitting opposite her during meals, silently contemplating her face illuminated in the lamplight. Was everything as he had hoped? Is anything ever as one hopes? He wasn't ungrateful to Laurence, not at all. More than anything, he wished to make her happy. And she was happy . . . sometimes even too readily, too easily pleased by a pretty outfit, a bouquet of fresh flowers, an unexpected gift. It was strange . . . he was grateful she was like that, but, at times, simultaneously wary, worried. He could not believe she was really so easily satisfied. In the early days of their marriage, he continually asked her: 'Are you really happy? Is everything exactly as you dreamed it would be?' He asked so often, sounding so sad that Laurence became irritated (but she was wiser than him and so said nothing). But then again, she had never felt that insatiable thirst for happiness, had she? Dear Laurence . . . He took her hand as she handed him the paper knife that he was looking for without realising it. (He wasn't even aware he'd been trying to find it.)

'You know what I want before I do,' he said.

She smiled.

'I watch you all the time. I read your face like a sailor who studies the shape of the clouds to predict calm waters or a storm.'

Such goodness and solicitude, her sweet disposition and even temper made her the best of women, he mused.

'My kind Laurence,' he said, sounding calm and affectionate. Why could he find nothing to say to her?

He had loved her so passionately! But she had yielded to him with modesty and mockery . . . Oh, a very slight mockery, but still . . . 'Your Oriental love, your wild love,' she would say. But he could only love passionately, madly, with total abandon, or . . . cease to love. And so they sat side by side, without saying a word.

'So you really like what that young woman does so much?' she asked, leaning towards the fire while slowly toying with her jade necklace. 'Did you see the painting on the easel when we went in? That low sky, those foreign men with curls falling down their cheeks, walking in the snow behind a coffin set diagonally across a sleigh?'

'A Jewish funeral,' said Harry.

'It's sinister, sordid, don't you think? And of course, it's not new. We've seen those brownish grey tones and that flowing silvery white a hundred times before.'

'But you can't imagine how real it is, how true,' said Harry, suddenly animated and leaning towards her. 'You shouldn't look at it as an art lover, do you see? Her technique is weak, but the way she paints affects me in a way that makes me forget the picture and allows me to rediscover myself, the real me. And that is undoubtedly what she is aiming for in her work. Along those strange, twisting paths, I find myself...'

He fell silent.

'And yet,' he continued, stroking Laurence's hair, 'I never actually saw anything like it. I belonged to a privileged class where the dead were buried with more pomp. And everyone took such care to make sure I was protected from any painful sight that I don't think I ever saw a dead person or animal throughout my entire childhood. When a funeral procession was passing by in the street, my governess had orders to keep me distracted by any means possible. Yet all I had to do was close my eyes to discover, within me, the sadness from which I was so carefully protected.'

'And now,' he thought, 'it's here again...'

He continued in a low, emotional voice:

'Yes, Laurence, even without having seen it, I know that it is true, true in its detail and especially in its immortal essence. The light snow that sometimes falls straight down because there isn't a hint of wind: that's surely the first snow in autumn; it disappears into the mud and puddles... That coffin, did you notice how it sat on the sleigh? Unsteady, diagonally... It hadn't been carefully placed, just thrown on like a useless object, like a stone... and the people who are following it, walking in the deep tracks, did you notice their faces? Coldness towards the dead man who will not be brought back to life by their tears, no hope whatsoever in everlasting life and, at the same time, such intense concentration, such passion . . . In the foreground, a child with dark eyes that dominate his face, and those thin little legs. I've seen so many little Jews who look like him! I, myself, who was cleaner and better dressed, I was a little Jew like him.'

She looked at him with a smile.

'But you're rambling, my poor Harry . . . I've seen photos of you when you were seven or eight, and I can assure you that you look nothing at all like the people in Madame Ada Sinner's works. You were a lovely little boy with beautiful curls. You looked healthy and very happy to be alive and held a magnificent Persian cat tight against your chest.'

They said nothing for a moment.

'And as a woman,' Harry asked, automatically continuing to stroke Laurence's hair, 'do you like her, as a woman?'

She hesitated, torn between an instinctive aversion to Ada and the desire to be loyal, which caused her to say something very fair:

'It's difficult to speak of her as a woman . . .'

'Yes, that's true, that's very true,' he exclaimed suddenly. 'I was wondering what there was about her that was different from other women: there's absolutely nothing feminine about her . . . She looks like a child . . . But you, my dear Laurence, if you suddenly found yourself on a deserted island, the very moment the confusion had ceased, you would go and collect some little feathers and seashells to dress yourself up for me, if I were with you, or in memory of me, if I were dead.'

'Of course. Thank goodness,' said Laurence. 'These young girls, these foreigners have no sense of style, no sensitivity, no feeling.'

'Is that what you think, my darling?'

'Ambition, well, that they have,' continued Laurence, sounding distinctly irritated. 'She cloaks her arrogance in a kind of modesty that I find quite despicable.'

Harry gently pushed her away, looked for a cigarette and carefully lit it.

'I don't believe,' he finally said, 'that her modesty is totally feigned. I see in it more an extreme mistrust of herself and of others.'

'Why mistrust? We accept her, treat her as an equal. Why do we deserve her mistrust? It's unfair.'

'We mustn't forget the unique situation of her life . . . The poverty, the loneliness and, at the same time, the awareness that she is, if not better than other people, then at least set apart from them; talent always does that to such unhappy souls when it takes hold of them. I'd like to help her, Laurence. People should meet her. We should invite some friends around to meet her one evening.'

'Here?' she asked, looking at him.

'Naturally.'

She didn't reply immediately. She got up from her chair, stood in front of the fire and stretched out her hands towards the flames.

'No, Harry.'

'Why not?'

'I for one do not wish to become a kind of patron to this young woman. I cannot vouch for her: I don't know her.'

'You talk about her as if it were a question of smuggling some tramp into a wealthy home so she can run off with the silver!' exclaimed Harry, angrily.

She looked at him coldly.

'How excitable you are, Harry!'

'And you reproach her for being mistrustful! You're the one who's mistrustful and unfair! Why must you assume these people are thieves?'

'Because I don't know them. You don't open your doors to people you don't know; do you understand? You bought her paintings, you talked about her, you introduced her to people. That's enough.'

'Charity, but given at the doorstep, at the entrance to the beautifully polished reception room, in the way it is given to peasants,' he said.

'Yes. Don't you understand that it's more a question of dignity than prudence? And I don't even want to go into the element of base curiosity that was just as odious to you as to me today! I only invite people into my home if I can treat them as friends, not as exotic animals.'

He stood up and took a few steps away from her.

'Laurence,' he said eventually, walking back over to her, 'I beg of you, don't refuse me this. I feel guilty about this child, I . . .'

'What do you mean? You don't even know her.'

'Yes, I do. I met her once . . . in my country, in *our* country . . . But Laurence, don't ask me to explain all that to you. You wouldn't, you couldn't understand. Trust me. Say you'll allow me to receive her in our home, to welcome her . . . It's very important, Laurence.'

'It's a whim.'

'So you refuse?'

'I don't like her. I don't like anything about her. Forgive me, Harry, but you've said this yourself many times: that mixture of arrogance and servility, which is specifically Jewish, is . . .'

She stopped.

'I didn't mean it,' she said.

He said nothing. His face had suddenly gone pale and tense; his lips were quivering.

'Harry, I detest men who are irritable,' she said with a harshness of which she was perhaps unaware. 'I'm used to you being more in control of yourself . . .'

'And I'm used to you being more tolerant . . .'

'Sometimes, you display an hysterical side of you that is . . . extremely unpleasant. I have often noticed it.'

He said nothing. He was shaking with rage and wounded pride. The look on his face was so strange, so full of hatred, that Laurence suddenly felt his hatred as a slap in the face, so she continued with an instinctively defensive reaction:

'I've noticed it in your son, without realising that he got it from you.'

It was true; the child would sometimes burst into tears or display excessive joy or anger, revealing an emotional instability that had often alarmed them both. With her confident woman's instinct, Laurence had struck upon the thing that would hurt Harry the most. But just as someone who has a gun pointing at his vital organs pushes it away, even though it might hit something else, something equally important, equally vulnerable, Harry was determined to change the subject, at any cost.

'Are you jealous?' he cried. 'Admit it! It would be better, more worthy of you!'

'Jealous? Of that ugly, shabbily dressed girl?'

'I didn't find her ugly,' he said slowly, feigning ingenuousness.

'If you find women like that attractive, I won't try to compete with them!'

'And yet, you're jealous.'

'No. A hundred times, a thousand times, no!'

'Do you know,' he suddenly shouted, 'that ever since she was a child, ever since *we* were children in *our* country, she's been in love with me? Do you remember that book someone sent to me shortly before we were married? We never knew where it came from. Do you know that she was the one who sent me that gift, because she wanted me to think about her, even for a moment, so I wouldn't think about you?'

'If she really did that then she's mad, and if you admire that, if you approve of that, then you're just as insane as she is.'

'Well I do! And I would have done exactly the same thing when I was in love with you!'

Both of them, pale and trembling, fell silent.

'Since you refuse to receive her here,' said Harry, harshly (when he was angry, his features seemed sharper; his colourless cheeks looked thinner, as if he were sucking them in), 'I shall ask my mother to have a party for her. You can either come or not, it's up to you.'

'She's married. Will you also invite her husband?'

'Why not?'

'But you don't know anything about him! You don't know where he comes from, what he's like. Are you going to associate with some stranger, some opportunist?'

'Don't you see that it is your attitude that pushes me into considering this stranger, this opportunist as a brother?'

'And me, your wife, as a foreigner, is that it? Be careful,' she continued with growing anger, 'this is about more than just receiving this young woman: it's about a deeper, more serious conflict.'

'Ah! So you understand that, do you?'

'So in spite of all my efforts,' she cried out sadly, 'I've never really understood what you were thinking, what you desired? That's what you're saying, isn't it? I thought you were happy.'

'No. I've never been happy, not for an hour, not for a single minute, never!'

In spite of himself, Harry's voice sounded shrill; his eyes were blazing. He hid his face in his hands and ran out of the room.

22

Ada was in a state of high anxiety and excitement as she put on her clothes. Her dress was simple, black. Fortunately, all women's dresses that year were shifts. She'd paid a lot of money for some silk stockings, and a collar and cuffs made of fine linen. How wonderful it felt to wear them! She studied her shoes for a long time: the heels were still straight, but the crêpe de Chine was rather worn at the edges. They had belonged to Lilla. For a week now Ada hadn't picked up a paintbrush, so she could cut out and make her dress. Her years as Aunt Raissa's apprentice hadn't been a total waste after all . . . She'd done a good job. Her hat was small, dark and made of felt; it was almost masculine but it showed off her face. The real problem was her coat – a horrible, threadbare coat – but she wasn't too worried about it because she was sure that no one kept their coats on once inside: that's how it was in Russia. Ben stood beside her and watched, silent and sarcastic.

'Let's go,' he said.

She looked away. The presence of Ben spoiled the game, that delightful game she'd engaged in ever since she'd received Harry's invitation, as if she were in some waking dream. Just as you rewind a film, so she had returned to the exact moment in time when her true life had been interrupted, her only true life, in spite of appearances: the instant when she had entered the large hall decorated with flowers and little French flags, holding Madame Mimi's hand, to be introduced to Harry. And now she had managed to sweep aside all the intervening years. She, Ada, had been invited to the Sinners' home; they were holding a reception in her honour, to introduce her to Parisian high society. Of course, even in the past, she would never have dreamt of such a thing. But in her mind, she gladly confused the past and the present, dream and reality. By some stroke of good fortune, even the day itself was the same as it had been back then: the air still, with a sense of sad resignation that soon it would snow. She walked alongside Ben and looked at him, wondering what he was thinking. Strange, enigmatic Ben.

'You won't ask them for anything, will you, Ben?' she asked, before they reached the Sinners' house, in a voice that was both defiant and pleading.

He smiled.

'You're so afraid of me!'

'You hate them!'

'I won't waste my time wondering if I love them or hate them. If they can be useful to me, that's enough.'

'But that's exactly what I don't want!'

'Really? And why not, my sweet? What are you going to tell them? Have I done anything wrong? I've earned my living, our living, as best I could. I'm not a murderer or a thief. Why would you want to stop me asking them for help and support, as in the past?'

'What do you want from them?'

'Your Harry could help me out . . . put in a good word for me to one of his uncles . . .'

'He won't want to.'

'Is that what you think? Why? I'm not going to ask them to

give me an allowance, just to hire me, offer me a job, the lowest possible, and I'm telling you, Ada, they'll take me.'

'More of your pipe dreams,' she murmured with pity and anger.

'No. I know these people. They can be as Europeanised and cultured as you like, but deep in their hearts, they still have a weakness for people who started out humbly, harshly, with difficulty, like they did. Because when all is said and done, those Sinners, with their racing stables and famous art collections, had fathers who were kids like me: starving, beaten, humiliated. And that creates a bond that is never forgotten, not one of race or blood, but a bond of tears. Do you understand? Why don't you want to let me try my luck, Ada? What else can I hope for on this earth, aside from money? I've already lost you.'

'What do you mean?'

'You love that damned boy.'

Profound pity filled Ada's heart. She looked at him with kindness.

'Ben, I've never been in love with you, you've always known that. But you're more than my husband, you're like my brother. I'm begging you to give up your idea of getting involved with these rich people and I . . . I'll go with you. I'll never see Harry again. What would be the point? He's married. He belongs to another woman. It was a dream, a childish fantasy. Come on. Let's go back home.'

'Ha!' Ben replied sadly, shrugging his shoulders. 'Our three destinies have been linked since we were children. There's nothing we can do about it.'

'And you don't want to let a chance to make yourself a fortune slip by,' she said with bitter resentment.

'I can't . . .' he said, between clenched teeth, 'let something slip away . . . that is within my reach. That's how I am . . . It's not my fault . . .'

They had arrived. They stopped for a moment, their hearts pounding. What courage it took for them to walk through the grand entrance, to enter the large private house and look the servant in the face as he opened the door for them.

Ada was terrified for a moment when she saw the women going into the formal drawing room wearing their furs. She quickly took off her coat and went into the room.

The elderly Madame Sinner shook her hand and said very loudly, 'We are related, are we not?'

Oh, if only Aunt Raissa could have heard this family tie she was so proud of proclaimed for all to hear.

'Yes, I think so, Madame,' Ada murmured. 'Distantly related . . .'

'And you've been living all alone, with no one, in this big city, without ever thinking you could come to us! But why?'

'I don't know. I suppose it never occurred to me, Madame.'

'Well, no harm done, since here you are now. You have some admirers who would like to meet you.'

So many curious faces! So many smiles! So many friends! And Harry walking towards her, at last. He could see that she was weary and embarrassed, close to tears. He took her by the arm and led her through the dining room which she had glimpsed, one summer's night, in the shimmering shadows as she watched the party, alone in the street. She had often tried to imagine this room, but in vain. He took her into a small empty sitting room.

'You're going to sit down here, calmly have a glass of champagne and look at all these people, without having to speak to them or smile at them, just as if you were at the theatre, all right?'

'I've already watched them as if I were at the theatre.'

'When?'

She explained.

'You've never been happy, you poor thing,' Harry remarked with a softness in his voice that was unusual for him.

She looked at him with an expression that was nearly disconcerting in its perceptive irony.

'Neither have you,' she said.

'What do you mean?'

'I'm free, yes, free. I can work all day long if I feel like it, or stay in bed and do nothing, and no one will worry or ask me if I'm ill. I can spend the whole afternoon strolling along the Seine to look at the colour of the water and I know that no one in all of Paris cares whether I'm dead or alive, whether I'll come home that night or not.'

'And you think that's a good thing?' he asked with curiosity.

'Well, it's the only good thing I've ever known, and can recommend to others,' she replied, smiling.

'What about your husband?'

'He's always busy, always travelling. I have no idea where he is or what he's doing for months at a time. But that's how he is and he's still my only friend.'

'You have another friend now,' he whispered, touching her hand.

He was deeply moved. With Laurence, he anxiously listened to every word she said, trying in vain to understand what she wasn't saying; but with Ada, words themselves were pointless: the subtleties in her voice, in her eyes, revealed to him the very essence of her soul.

Ben paced back and forth past the open door. He made his way through the dazzling crowd as if he were at a train station. His frizzy hair, burning eyes, pale cheeks and sharp features made him look striking and strange.

When he recognised Harry, he headed towards him. Ada walked away, back into the drawing room. People spoke to her and she replied shyly. But she never took her eyes off Harry and Ben. A few moments later, she saw an older man with yellowish skin, a hooked nose and large, dark eyes go over to them. She guessed he was one of Harry's uncles. So, once again, Ben's determination, passion and arrogance had got him what he wanted.

'But me too,' she thought. She looked once more at everything around her with curiosity and surprise. The women were beautiful and dazzling, the men elegant, with light, lively voices. Yet, in spite of that, this reception at the Sinners' home and the afternoon tea dance she had once watched from a distance were as different from each other as reality is to a dream.

She realised that Harry had come to stand beside her.

'Do you like all this?' he asked her.

'Yes, but . . .' She sighed, sadly. 'Somehow, it was even better seen from below!'

23

Ben was on his way back from Brussels. It was the night before a religious holiday and the train was full of priests and children going on a pilgrimage in the north of France. Ben had spent the several hours of the journey in the corridor, sitting on a suitcase that did not belong to him and sleeping soundly, his head knocking against the metal side of the carriage every time the train lurched. He did not feel tiredness any more than he felt fear, hunger or despair. Tiredness never really took hold of him, or rather it over-stimulated him to such an extent that he forgot about his frail body. Certain extreme emotions seemed literally to thrust him outside himself, endowing him with superhuman agility and stamina.

They were approaching Paris; he woke up. He looked at the people in the neighbouring carriages with scornful curiosity. How slow they were. How heavy. They dragged women, children, packages behind them. Even people like him who had a profession that sent them constantly roaming from city to city, from country to country – travelling salesmen, stallholders, actors on tour – even they looked confused, weighed down, battered, while to him, none of it mattered at all. Everywhere was the same to him; he wandered indifferently from place to place, left each behind with no regrets.

Ever since he was a child, he had been taught and made to feel that he belonged to nothing, to no one. Well, fine! *They* had got what they wanted. (Ben thought of the rest of the world as *they*, *them*, not exactly as enemies but not as friends either, simply as incomprehensible creatures.) Yes, they had achieved their goal in turning him into a wonderfully free person, unfettered by any obstacles. It was just as well that nothing meant anything to him because if ever the fever of passion took hold of Ben, it was not easily satisfied, not easily forgotten.

He could be up and ready in a second, while the others were still fishing around for their tickets, rounding up their children, calling out to their friends, putting the collars on their dogs. He was travelling with no luggage, just a pair of old pyjamas stuffed into his pocket, along with a bit of soap wrapped in newspaper; he needed nothing more. That way, he was always first, always ready to snatch the deal away from his rivals. And how they would complain afterwards. How unfair they were! All they had to do was copy him! Did he waste his time languishing in his wife's arms, drinking his coffee in bed, stroking the cat, fiddling with the dials on the radio, spending two hours politely eating some slowly cooked meal like the French? Not that he looked down on such habits. Quite the contrary. But they were foreign and incomprehensible to him. He had to hurry, pursue something he wanted, triumph over everyone else, because he knew that once beaten, he might as well be dead. Who cared about Ben? Who would help Ben up if he fell to the ground? Who would dress his wounds? Only Ada . . . and even then, it wouldn't be out of love – no one loved Ben – it would be out of a bond, out of pity. As for the others . . . Perhaps everything might change now. He was on his way to becoming rich: the wealthy Sinners were taking an interest in him. Oh, they were cautious, haughty towards him . . . but he didn't care if people respected him or not. When old Salomon, to whom he was related after all, didn't even ask him to sit down when he went to see him, that didn't bother him a bit. All he asked was for them to throw him a bone from time to time. He worked tirelessly, for he knew that the two old men were keeping an eye on him. He had sensed it before he'd even met them. Hardened as they were by time and weakened by luxury, they retained enough of their memories to recall their origins, and Ben's passion, his eagerness, appealed to some very ancient tendency within them, even though they might not be conscious of it, even though they might even be ashamed of it, but one that had more life than their dried-out old bodies. Oh, to manage to go even further, to get inside the business, to see how it worked, discover its secrets! Wasn't he, Ben, more worthy of being their heir than Harry, that boy he so despised?

'Slow down,' Ben whispered to himself, 'slow down.'

It was like putting a leash on an excited animal. Yet his longing for immediate success, his passion, was both his strength and his weakness. In his mind, he could already see himself sitting at the place of honour, next to Isaac and Salomon, instead of Harry. And so many deals would be possible, so many wonderful triumphs! The world was no longer the same, and in this changing universe, what was the point of prudently saving, sacrificing everything out of concern for the opinion of society and superficial vanity? Pulling off deals quickly, audaciously, snapping up millions overnight and using the money to speculate again, that's what you had to do! That's what he, Ben, wanted to do! No swindling, no! Deals. Taking a chance on countries in a state of chaos, in Europe or Asia . . . lending them money and getting mines, oil fields, concessions for building railroads in exchange. That was how to get rich! In his third-class carriage, swaying between the two walls, amid the smoke, the noise, the night, the winter rain, in the train station of a suburb, Ben fantasised about enormous deals, imagined financial schemes just as an artist creates a universe purely from his imagination. He alone understood what he was capable of, what he was worth. He had already conned so many others, known so many different people; he had the experience of an old man. Perhaps his race also played a part? Perhaps he felt, like all Jews, that vague and slightly frightening feeling of carrying within oneself a past that was heavier than the past of most men. At times when someone else might need to learn something, he, Ben, was remembering it – at least, that's what he believed.

Paris, at last! He jumped off the train. The station was heaving with people; he was the first to get outside because he knew how to slip in between the hurrying crowds, how to find the weak spot in a barrier, push through it, instinctively working out the shortest route. He wore an old hat and shabby raincoat. His hair fell in thick, dark little curls over his forehead. He had an unpleasant face: he'd always known that. Not that he was ugly, but his face was so thin that his features seemed to merge, as if there was not enough room for them all. His fine, reddish eyebrows met above his nose; his pinched, animated nostrils almost touched his upper lip; his mouth and chin were crowded together, and his straight teeth were set almost one on top of each other. His face never looked at peace. It quivered constantly, like rippling water. When he spoke, ten gestures accompanied each word, and each movement was the manifestation of an emotion pushed to the extreme: anger, joy, curiosity, anxiety – none of these was ever exhibited as they were by other people, in large waves of emotion, but rather by short little passionate ripples, which made his features look perpetually in conflict over a thousand contradictory thoughts. He was forced to stop for a moment; he had crossed the street and gone down into the metro. But the doors had just shut in front of him. That moment of forced stillness seemed to cause him to suffer. He blushed, went white, bit his nails, took off his hat, twisted it, put it back on his head, and finally rushed towards the second-class carriage as if his life depended on it.

He said nothing, but his lips were moving; he tapped his agile fingers on his knees and against the dark window of the train. He leapt out on to the platform. He was home. He checked the time: past midnight. He went into the lodging house and opened the door to his rooms. 'Ada!' he called out. No one replied, but someone was stretched out on the settee in the studio. When she had pulled herself up into a sitting position, he recognised Madame Mimi's white hair, set in old-fashioned little curlers.

'Where's Ada?'

She was wearing a silk dressing gown with leaves on it over her nightclothes; she modestly closed it around her thin legs. She would never have agreed, not for anything in the world, to be seen in her nightdress; even her curlers were artistically arranged and set with little orange ribbons.

'You gave me quite a shock, my dear boy,' she sighed. Her eyes, which age had begun to cloud over but which were still often very perceptive, studied Ben with a look that was simultaneously shrewd and uncertain, as if she were reluctant to speak before she had read his expression.

'Are you sleeping here now?'

'Yes. Is that all right with you? Ada was all alone . . .'

'Where is she?'

Madame Mimi stood up and switched on the lamp.

'Have you had any dinner? I'm afraid there isn't much here . . .'

'I asked you where Ada is.'

'At a concert, my dear.'

He didn't ask 'With whom?' He threw his hat on to a chair and sat down.

'Have you had any dinner?' Madame Mimi asked again.

'I had a sandwich and a beer.'

'Ah, you never change, not you . . . Always being chased by the devil! I'll heat up some soup for you.'

'All right . . . no, I'm not hungry . . . if you want to,' he murmured.

She went out. He noticed that the room was filled with the smell of roses. He turned around: yes, there was a bouquet. Never had he seen such beautiful flowers. He tried to find the card that must have come with the delivery. Nothing. A look of savage, painful irony came across his face. Such cruel mockery, directed inwards: no one could inflict it better than he himself. It mixed with his insol-ence and pride in a strange way. In a flash, he could call up a thousand poisoned arrows that ripped through him, one by one. He walked over to the flowers and touched them shyly; they fascinated him. Such an intoxicating perfume! He leaned his burning cheek in towards one of them and sighed with pleasure at the feel of the tightly closed, firm little rose against his skin.

Madame Mimi came into the room carrying a tray. 'Leave the flowers alone, Ben,' she cried.

He moved away, looking at her with a sly, stubborn expression, like a child who's been beaten.

'I'm not hungry,' he grunted.

'Then go to bed.'

He sat down again without replying.

She took the soup he hadn't touched and began slowly to drink it, peering over the top of the cup and flashing him a look that was as quick and piercing as a dart.

'They're beautiful flowers, aren't they? In the past, deep red roses were my favourites. In the past, the Prince . . . But what am I saying? All that is so long ago, forgotten . . . Where are those rose gardens now where I used to pick flowers to pin on my dresses? Roses like those. You know, I even decorated my horses with them, in Cannes . . . Yes, at the flower show, I had roses sewn on to my parasol and on to the horses' blinkers . . . What are you going to do? Do you intend to sit there opposite me all night, without moving?'

'Go to bed!'

'In front of a young man! Well, I never! Hand me the cards.'

He automatically shuffled them and dealt them out for a game. They played for a while in silence.

'Are you jealous?' she asked at last.

He said nothing.

'I thought you were above all such fine feelings, Ben . . .'

'Do you know what she wants to do now? Is she going to leave me?'

He was speaking quietly, without looking at her. He seemed calm, but drops of sweat were running down his cheeks; he wiped them away with the back of his hand.

'I can't breathe in here,' he said suddenly, throwing down his cards.

It was true that the small room was stifling. The windows must not have been opened all day and the radiators were burning hot. It meant that Ada hadn't spent a single hour there since yesterday: she could only bear living in rooms that were icy cold.

'Does she want to leave me, Madame Mimi?'

'She hasn't spoken to me about you.'

'So she's finally got what she wanted,' he said softly, sounding bitter.

Madame Mimi crossed her hands over her chest, and like an old soothsayer entering into a trance, she began speaking in a deep voice, one that scarcely resembled her usual lively, sharp tone. It was always startling to hear it, just as a certain cooing of doves is surprising in its harshness:

'Oh, how alike you two are . . . Neither of you can calmly walk past a closed door without cunningly, or forcefully, trying to get in where God has forbidden you to go. You remain patient! You wait for an opportunity, or you bang on the door even harder until someone opens it . . . You've always been like that, Ben, and your wife is just the same. That's how you got *her*, and that's how she . . .'

Ben closed his eyes. The old woman's words sounded like bees buzzing in the distance. He had never experienced that.

'Is she going to leave me?'

'Listen to me,' said Madame Mimi, leaning towards him and taking his hands in hers – they were as dry and light as a bird's – 'You have always known that she didn't love you. She's not the right girl for you. Ada is special . . .'

'I'm special too,' he said with bitter pride. 'Just give me a few years and I'll be in charge of many things and many people who now treat me like the mud on their shoes.'

'She doesn't love you.'

'She's as cold as stone,' he whispered.

'No, Ben.'

'If she would only . . . stay with me . . . I wouldn't ask anything else . . . I would let her . . . be with Harry . . . The way these sophisticated people behave sometimes has its uses,' he said, sounding pained and sarcastic, 'but it's the idea of losing her that's . . . unbearable. She's always been with me. You know that's true . . . We even used to sleep in the same room. I used to wake up and look at her black hair while she was in bed . . . We used to walk through the streets of the lower town together . . . I never really felt unhappy or alone because I knew that she was with me. She can't leave me.'

'Be quiet,' said Madame Mimi. 'They're home.'

24

Ada had come in with Harry. They were both talking loudly and laughing. It was the laughter that both angered Ben and astonished him: he had so rarely heard Ada laugh. She was always silent and distant, lost in her daydreams. She was back down on earth now, thought Ben, watching her. She was dressed as simply as ever, almost shabbily, but she seemed happy, younger and more feminine, her face illuminated by an intense yet soft light that disappeared the moment she saw Ben.

The two men eyed each other contemptuously, in silence.

'I'm back now,' said Ben. 'Get out.'

Harry took Ada by the shoulder.

'Let's go, Ada. It's better to get this over with, once and for all.'

Until now, Ben had remained calm. When he heard the way Harry said 'Ada', he flew into a rage. It was the French pronunciation, with the accent on the last letter, which Ben found affected and almost insulting. He shouted out his fury in curses and insults; the words he spoke were interspersed with Yiddish and Russian: Harry barely understood them. To Harry, there was something repugnant and grotesque in the way he swore, gesticulating wildly in an outburst of hatred. He immediately thought of the expression of horror there had been on Laurence's face when she'd called him hysterical. These howls of passion, these frenzied calls to a vengeful god came from a different world.

'I want to watch you die!' shouted Ben. 'I hope your body is ripped to shreds! I hope you have no peace, no rest, no easy death! I curse you and all your descendants! I curse all your sons!'

'Be quiet!' Harry shouted harshly. 'We're not in a ghetto in the Ukraine any more!'

'But you came out of that ghetto just like I did, just like her! If you only knew how much I hate you! You who look down on us from on high, who despise us, who refuse to have anything in common with the Jewish scum. Wait a bit! Just wait! You'll be considered part of that scum again one day. And you'll be dragged back into it, you who got out, you who thought you'd escaped. I've always hated you so much. For all the reasons that made Ada love you. Because you were rich! Because you wore clean clothes! Because you were happy! But just you wait. We'll see which one of us ends up happier, which one of us has more money: you, rich and spoiled ever since you were a child, or me, a poor, miserable Jew. Perhaps one day, Ada, you'll realise what you lost in me. Millions! I could have given you millions, if you'd only been patient enough to wait.'

'Be quiet now, you dirty little opportunist,' shouted Harry. 'How can you not understand how horrible it is to talk about money, to bring money into this?'

'Oh how I hate all your European pretensions! What you call success, victory, love, hatred, is what I call money. It's just a different word for the same things. Both our ancestors talked this way. It's our own language. You know very well why she fell in love with you. Because you had a clean collar and cuffs that day we went to your house for the first time, for our sins, while I, I was splattered with dust and blood. And it was money that made the difference. It's not as if you were from a different bloodline, a different race . . . Well, in those days I would have said to myself:

"Ben, my poor boy, you're nothing but mud, you are, but him, he's a prince. Better get out." But you're not a prince! Look at yourself. You have my hooked nose, my frizzy hair, you're weak and frail, as hungry and miserable as I am . . . Hungry for other things, perhaps, but hungry all the same and not fulfilled and satisfied like other people . . . I could have been you and you could have been me. Ada! Why do you prefer him to me? Take a good look. Look at us carefully. Him and me, me and him, we're cut from the same cloth. We're brothers.'

'No, no, it isn't true,' said Harry, hiding his face in his hands.

'Look, just look at him! Is that the kind of gesture a European would make? He's afraid to look at me. He's afraid of seeing his own reflection. Ada, stay with me! I don't care about wounded pride or any of your sophisticated stupidity. I understand what it means to long for something, to nurture a passion within you since childhood. Good for you if you've managed to get what you want for once.'

'Ben, I've never loved you. You think that we are like you, Ben, but you're the one who sees yourself wherever you look. I don't need money, Ben; I don't even need happiness. I want to live in a different way, can you understand that? I want to experience a kind of life that is not just work and longing, but tranquillity, tenderness, quiet pleasures. You shout, you curse, you're full of spite and bitterness; you hurt other people more than you hurt yourself. Poor Ben, let me go. Don't be stubborn. Oh, Ben, listen to me . . .'

Harry crossed his arms and said nothing; he left them alone together. In spite of everything, the two of them spoke the same language. Ada had sat down next to Ben; she'd put her arm around his long, frail neck; it was too long, too frail. Harry couldn't hear what she was whispering in Ben's ear. Their cheeks were touching. Their hair merged into a single mass. Anxiously Harry touched his own face. He knew that he looked like Ben, yet (and this was the snag) they had very few features in common; his other features were as different from Ben as from Laurence herself. But no one would ever believe it. Never. He would be forever rejected by both sides, endlessly snubbed by each, continually paying for the sins that Ben might commit. But his bitterness, his angry resignation could have been Ben's. He felt as if some stranger's body had been attached to his own and that he would never succeed in tearing it away without destroying his own flesh.

'I'm begging you,' he cried in anguish, 'leave him be. Come on, Ada, let's go!'

She stood up. Ben grabbed her by the shoulders. Harry thought he was going to hit her; he leapt forward, but all Ben did was take Ada's face in his hands and stare at her the way you stare at someone who has died before closing the cover of the casket. Then he pushed her away, ran out of the room and disappeared.

25

One May morning, two years later, Isaac and Salomon Sinner, the current owners of the bank, were expecting their nephew Harry. They got up late, bathed and scrubbed their old, delicate bodies. They had their nails done by their private manicurists, beautiful young women whom they could no longer embrace: they simply watched them from a distance with a sense of pleasure mixed with annoyance and regret, the way you look at flowers behind a window. They dressed meticulously, with infinite care, and finally swathed their dry carcasses in dressing gowns which, through the richness of their colours and the perfection of their cut, were the triumph of two combined arts: the art of the Orient and the art of London. This had always been the more or less conscious goal of their ambition: to offer through their appearance a subtle combination of propriety and luxury. Up until now, everything about them had been impeccably proper, but with a hint of foreignness, like the perfume given off by certain tropical hardwoods. They were extraordinarily alike: thin and slight of frame with curly white hair, dark circles under their eyes and complexions that age had changed from swarthy to yellowish.

They had worked very hard. They were born at a time when their father, the famous elderly Sinner, idol and role model of the Ukrainian Jews, had not yet built up his formidable fortune. They were the two eldest sons, the ones who had to be taught to work hard early on – the younger ones were shown some indulgence, but the older ones were there before anyone could be spoiled, before anyone had been softened by extreme security and luxury. They were the heirs apparent, destined only for responsibilities in life and none of its privileges. They had left Russia with limited means, for the money earned by their father had been endlessly speculated, constantly jeopardised, gambled with time and time again with infinite good fortune but also extremely dangerously. They knew almost as well as their father that they could count on no one if they failed. Of course, they could always go back to the Ukraine where they would have food and a roof over their heads, but they would have no active participation in the company business: the elderly Sinner refused to die.

But in Europe, they had succeeded. They founded a small bank that, in the beginning, had been nothing more than the slave of the distant, colossal enterprises of their father, but which had gradually grown . . . Ah, they had the right to be proud! In its heyday, kings came to beg for money from their company. Thanks to their patient efforts, it had expanded and prospered. Now it lived on by virtue of its own merits, like a human life form. The two brothers were old; their presence in the immense presidential office every day, from two o'clock to four o'clock, no longer had any real significance, any real importance to the carrying out of business than the great full-length portrait of their father hanging on the wall. Yet in spite of everything, they were revered amongst their closest collaborators, in the way that old bottles of wine, covered in dust and spiders' webs are revered. Only when the bottles are opened, the wax seal removed, the wine poured into glasses and tasted does it become evident that time, after improving the wine for so long, has ended up spoiling it: all its flavour has gone, and the only thing to do now is throw it away.

Were they aware of this? Only Harry had often asked himself that question. He found them sitting opposite one another in the dining room. He always felt uneasy when he went there, as if it were some vast cemetery. It was covered in so many expensive paintings that you could barely see the rich purple colour of the walls. His uncles were holding cups in their swarthy hands, in exactly the same pose; they still drank Turkish coffee in spite of their age, their heart palpitations and their insomnia. In their gold and scarlet dressing gowns, they looked like two old icons from ancient times. Did they actually understand that they no longer had any real power? That they had willingly locked themselves away in a retreat where the only people they received were opportunists or servants? That they had gradually lost contact with the outside world? That they lived as if the world was the same as it had been before 1914, and with the same problems? Did they still see their somnambulant state as wisdom, their inertia as prudence, their lack of imagination as experience? For Harry firmly believed that they lacked imagination. Perhaps because he had known them since childhood, he had never noticed that beneath their aloof expression burned the fire of the passionate soul with which all the Sinners, every last one of them, had been afflicted, to a greater or lesser extent . . .

The lack of understanding between these two generations had been pushed to an extreme. To Harry, his uncles appeared to have no human traits left; in their eyes, Harry was their heir, in the Oriental sense of the word: someone who would stop at nothing, so the old men thought, to overthrow them and steal everything they had. Harry might feign detachment and indifference, but that was so he could trick them better. He might pretend to have a cynical dislike of business: he thought it the best way to get rid of them. But they were still strong enough to keep power firmly in their hands. Let him wait! *They* had been forced to wait a very long time for their father to die. They had waited so long that when they finally found themselves in complete control of their fortune, they were already fifty-two, which was perhaps the reason why they had never forgiven Harry: he was still only a child when he inherited his share of his grandfather's estate. Fortunately, they were his trustees: they took everything. Later on, when it was time to account for Harry's funds, who would have the nerve to deny these two venerable, elderly men the right to keep the money they had managed with such skill? And besides, there was the bank. Harry would inherit the bank. In the meantime, they shrouded themselves in impenetrable secrecy. They jealously engaged spies, confidence men, an entire entourage of people whose function was to keep Harry as far away as possible from involvement in the business. Two old painted icons perhaps, but no one could touch them without being accused of madness or sacrilege; their old hands were simultaneously delicate and dangerous. Their frailty itself was menacing. How could anyone do battle with these fragile, brittle old men? In their brilliantly coloured dressing gowns, they resembled two dead butterflies.

Harry did not feel the loathing towards them that they believed he did. Harry found them odd, irritating and touching, all at once. They both stretched out their hands to him with the same cold gesture. Isaac indicated that he should sit down; Salomon pointed out to the servant a chink in the curtain that was letting in a ray of sunshine. It was adjusted, and the room was bathed in the soft, rich, reddish glow of wine or roses. A servant silently entered the room carrying the platter of fresh fruit that his masters ate for breakfast, to purify their sluggish blood, thickened by age. Isaac allowed himself to be served with the serenity of a god on Mount Olympus, accepting chilled golden grapes served from the end of long antique scissors, just as certain exotic birds accept food placed in their beaks. Salomon was more alert; life still manifested itself in him through gestures of impatience and mistrust. He watched every move the servant made; frowning, he pointed out that two of the grapes had little rust-coloured spots. He pushed his plate away and it was immediately removed and replaced by another made of bright-green porcelain and full of beautiful strawberries. The entire set of dishes was valuable and rare.

'Sad old things,' thought Harry.

He refused their offer of fruit and coffee but waited patiently while his uncles finished their breakfast, for he knew that it was impossible to speak to them and have any chance of them listening until they had satisfied their finicky appetites. Salomon was now slowly eating his strawberries rolled in sugar. You could tell him apart from his brother by the shape of his nose: the bridge was very thin and looked broken in two places, and its sharp point almost touched his lips, while Isaac's nose hung heavily down, like some exotic fruit. They both had large, almond-shaped eyes, like the young men in Persian miniatures. They seemed to sense that Harry was impatient, even though experience had taught him to hide it as best he could. They made the slow, ceremonial meal last as long as possible. Finally, Salomon wiped his hands on a green linen napkin, and Isaac gestured that he would take the few letters that had been opened and sorted by their secretaries and placed in a neat stack, like toast on a gilt platter.

This was the final ritual. Holding the paper knife at the height of his eyebrow, Isaac glanced over the pages he'd already read; everything that was important or essential had already been removed. Then he dropped the letters and gave a bored sigh. Salomon was skimming through the morning papers.

In the reddish darkness of the stuffy dining room, breathing in the sweet smell of fruit and the vague aroma of spices and ginger that seemed to linger around his uncles, Harry had to fight a strange feeling of drowsiness. He had often felt this. The presence of these old men acted upon him like a drug; their slow gestures and monotonous voices cast a sort of spell. 'We are very old, very wise,' they seemed to be saying. 'What do you think you can teach us? We have seen the beginning of things and we shall see their end.'

Harry began speaking more quickly, more nervously than he would have liked.

'Uncle,' he said (he always instinctively spoke to Salomon, as he was the one who had retained a touch of humanity), 'Uncle, is it true that we have added two more countries to the list of governments you've loaned money to in the past few years?'

Neither of the old men replied. Salomon closed his *Figaro* interminably slowly and put it down on his empty plate. A bee had somehow managed to infiltrate the carefully sealed room and was buzzing about, attracted by the smell of strawberries. Isaac swung at it nervously with the paper knife he was holding.

'It's the flowers on the terrace that attracts them. You'll never believe me, but yesterday, in my room, I heard quite distinctly a mosquito humming right near my bed ... At the beginning of May! In Paris ...'

Salomon turned towards his nephew.

'Maybe you could get rid of it? You're an agile young man,' he said in the sarcastic, melancholy tone of voice he used when speaking to his nephew, as if each word were accompanied by the thought: 'All we're good for now is to be thrown on to the fire, is that what you think, young man? Well then, set out the logs, fan the flames, but don't be surprised if there is still some fight left in us!'

'Leave it alone,' Harry said curtly. 'It won't hurt you. You haven't answered my question,' he said after a moment's silence.

'What were you saying, dear boy? I didn't hear you properly, forgive me.'

Harry stood up and began pacing around the room under the watchful eyes of his uncles.

'I am worried about the business,' he said. 'For some time now, too much seems to have been happening at once. I would even go so far as to say that I find the profits themselves worrying, completely out of proportion.'

'Since when has the younger generation complained about an established enterprise, one moreover that it is destined to inherit, adapting to modern times and trying to make money in any way it can?'

'I have seen the names of all the countries to which we have given loans, in some form or other,' said Harry. 'It is over-whelming. All the countries in Europe and the Orient are on the list, especially in the Orient, and that is what I find worrying.'

'Have you considered the advantages we get in return?' Isaac said quietly. 'We have taken control of some extremely important institutions. In exchange, the governments we support have conceded solid, appreciable assets to us . . . Leave it to us to run things, Harry. Up until now you haven't had any complaints about the way we've managed the business.'

'It's not you I'm worried about. For two years now, you've placed all your trust in a petty opportunist whom we know nothing about . . . and all these foreign loans, all these complicated schemes bear the mark of a spirit that is not our own . . .'

'Who might that be?' asked Salomon. 'This "family spirit" you talk of could not have found anyone more suitable than your cousin, and I don't mind telling you, Harry, that if your grand-father were to return to this world, he would recognise himself in your cousin and not in you.'

'But until now, we haven't needed anyone else to grow and prosper.'

'No, but neither the behaviour nor the activities of the company have changed as much as you think, Harry. We were lending vast sums of money to kings long before you were even born.'

'But not like this,' said Harry, shaking his head impatiently, 'not like this. Don't take me for a child. I know what I'm talking about. For the past two years, we've been involved in everything, in gold mines and iron ore, in weapons and platinum ... just like the brokers in the ghetto who couldn't care less whether they bought and sold raisins from Smyrna or silk from Turkistan. And one day, the whole mad structure will collapse and fall on to my shoulders, mine and mine alone!'

'They are quite delicate shoulders, it must be said, but we hope to live for a few more years yet,' said Isaac, 'and hopefully, we'll only die when the heir to our company has shown himself worthy of succeeding us.'

'I wonder,' thought Harry, 'if they're saying such pompous things tongue in cheek or out of spite, in the way that you hand a child the most common flower, the easiest to pick, rather than going to the trouble of finding him something rarer. Or are they actually sincere? The truth is, I'd have to jump on their old bodies and give them a good shake to get to the bottom of things, to save them – and myself. My cousin Ben wouldn't flinch at doing such a thing, but of course, I'm too civilised.'

'The Delarchers are extremely concerned about us as well, or so it seems,' Salomon remarked. 'Your father-in-law has said more or less the same thing to me.'

'And what did you tell him?'

Salomon smiled; the smile appeared then disappeared from his lips like a soft ripple on the murky water of a lake.

'What was the point of saying anything?'

Harry could just picture him opposite the elderly Delarcher: he imagined his sly smile and the way he shaded his eyes with his hand, as if protecting them from some harsh light.

'This air of secrecy around you is the cause of much hatred,' Harry murmured.

His uncle held his head up high; for just a second, a look of pride and mockery gave his features the semblance of youthfulness.

'Do you think you're frightening me? You poor child! Have I ever known anything but hatred? It has been one of the formative elements of my life. Are fish afraid of the water?'

'I truly believe,' Harry said suddenly, 'that you are reliving your finest moments through another person . . .'

They said nothing; they disliked being understood.

The sun had gone behind a cloud and the luxurious, stifling room was thrown into shadow; even the silvery reflections from the coffee pot had lost their glow. The elderly Salomon gestured to a servant who had entered; he helped the old man get up. One after the other, the shimmering dressing gowns disappeared, leaving Harry alone.

26

'We'd be better off apart,' said Laurence, one Sunday in spring.

She and Harry had spent the whole day behind closed doors involved in an intense discussion: the saddest one a married couple can have, with no shouting, no tears and no hope of understanding one another. The servants strained to listen, but the only sounds they heard were whispers and, now and again, Laurence's sad, trembling voice saying over and over again, 'I can't bear it. We'd be better off apart.'

They had already agreed this several months before when Laurence had learned from her older sisters – who could smell a scandal in the distance the way a hunting dog follows the scent of a partridge – that Harry was keeping 'that woman'. But that time she had cried and heaped reproach upon her husband; he had fought back, dragged up past grievances. The result was that their quarrel was like an illness – serious but not fatal – and the next day, a shaky reconciliation had been made. But just as the patient who thinks he has been cured still has deadly germs in his body, there remained between the husband and wife a kind of mistrust, a feeling of troubled embarrassment that gradually poisoned every moment they spent together.

The night before, Laurence had asked Harry if he would agree to accept an invitation to go with her on a cruise. He had said no.

They hadn't spoken of Ada since their first argument, and Harry now realised that his wife had not given up hope of seeing him and Ada separate.

What Harry didn't understand was the fierceness of Laurence's hope. She did not beat her fists against a locked door the way Ada did, but instead behaved like her provincial ancestors, patiently mending lace, refusing to give up, even though others might think the lace irreparable. Those ancestors of hers knew that with hard work and long, sleepless nights, anything could be mended, cleaned, made to look like new: all it took was time and effort. Laurence thought he would either end the affair or become more indifferent, but the truth was, as she bitterly admitted to herself, that Ada had taken her place. Laurence was not afraid of Harry having a mistress; she was afraid that Ada had become his friend. When Harry came home to her, it was not as an exhausted man who had spent his passion and sought the bland tranquillity of married life. She could have forgiven him that: hadn't she seen her mother welcome home her father the same way? But Harry returned as if he had left his haven of peace to be thrown into a stormy sea. That was what she could not understand. Hadn't she done her very best after the first and only scene never to raise her voice, never complain she was being neglected, never ask for promises or reassurance? But whenever he was with Laurence, he seemed to be afraid he'd be the victim of some blow, some injury. Even his face, which was paler and calmer when he'd just left Ada, turned weary and gloomy after he'd been in the family home for only a few moments.

Her only salvation was to believe in her own victory, but that was impossible.

An incident that happened that very day, and which had nothing to do with Harry's affair, suddenly put an end to her long, patient, but ultimately fruitless efforts. On the first Thursday of every month, their child was taken to see the elderly Madame Sinner. Laurence would sometimes go to collect the child herself, for she had a very strong sense of duty. Today, she found the old woman in a state: the child had fallen, his knee was bleeding and the Swiss governess had refused to do anything but clean his knee with a bit of cold water, laughing scornfully at all the disinfectants, powders and creams that the panicky grandmother had offered. Laurence's little boy had ended up panicking himself, and becoming hysterical.

'Wash his hands and face and take him home,' Laurence told the Swiss nanny. 'And he's not to have any dessert tonight to teach him not to cry over nothing.'

Once the child had gone, the two women remained alone in the room, staring at each other in silence.

'I would be very grateful, Madame,' Laurence finally said, coldly, 'if you would not encourage the child's tendency to think he is worse off than he is. He is already too sensitive.'

'You are a terrible mother,' thought the old woman, trembling with fury and looking daggers at Laurence. 'You horrible creature! Oh, if only I could take my beloved grandson from you and never set eyes on you again!'

Out loud, however, in the sweet tone of voice that drove Laurence mad, she said, 'Don't you think he's a little young to be brought up so strictly?'

'No, I do not,' Laurence replied curtly.

'His father, at his age . . .'

'You brought him up according to the customs of your country and your race, but . . .'

Her mother-in-law's long, powdered face, too pale for her dark eyes, became distorted with rage.

'He was brought up to be happy! And he isn't happy!'

'Yes, but I want to raise my son,' Laurence said quietly, 'to be strong, to make sacrifices, to be master of his body and soul, do you understand?'

'It's easy for her to talk that way,' thought the old woman, 'to imagine that kind of future for your children when you know that nothing and no one can harm them. But I . . . I had to make sure my child survived at all costs, and before me thousands of women of my race had to protect their children from being abused, from hunger, from unjust hatred, epidemics, poverty . . . We have been terrified by that, scarred by that, and for ever. But how can this foreigner, this young woman from a fortunate background possibly understand me?'

A strange weakness had overwhelmed Laurence. Afterwards, she would never understand why it was to this woman, whom she hated with all her heart, that she admitted what up until now she had not even been able to confide to her own mother:

'Madame, I do not know whether what I am about to tell you will pain you or on the contrary bring you joy, for you have never liked me. I wish to leave Harry.'

Madame Sinner affected surprise, but in so obviously false a way, so dramatically, that Laurence turned pale.

'You aren't surprised then?' she asked. 'Did you already know? Did your son tell you?'

'No, no, I swear to you!' protested the old lady, sincerely this time. 'May God strike me down where I stand! May I never again see my son if I am lying . . .'

'But you did know, didn't you?'

'Yes,' she murmured. 'Don't you see?' she said even more quietly. 'He's my son . . . How can he hide anything from me? However hard he tries, I can read everything in his face.'

'So you also know that he . . . that . . . that woman . . .'

'Yes, I know . . .'

'You must be happy,' cried Laurence, 'happy finally to see him with one of your own . . .'

'Me? Happy?'

This time there was no doubting her sincerity; she was shaking with fury.

'A simple girl from the slums! It's the worst thing that could possibly happen. It's what I've feared all my life. I wanted to save him from that poverty, that misery, that curse! But it was all in vain! And now, he's sunk down to their level . . .'

'Whose level?'

'Those people . . . those opportunists. They're bad luck, I'm telling you, but you can't get away from them. They're going to drag us down with them.'

Laurence recalled those words while she was talking to Harry. After her visit to her mother-in-law, she clearly saw that it was useless to keep on fighting: if Harry was not attracted to the woman out of passion or because of his family, then it was because of some obscure blood tie against which she was powerless. She could do everything in her power to try to win back her husband, but it would all be in vain. Despite all the civil and religious rites, he was not really her husband: he belonged to another woman, a woman whose destiny was linked to his for all eternity.

'There's nothing I can do,' she thought.

That was when she said, 'We'd be better off apart.'

The servants heard nothing from behind the double doors and thick curtains. But given the particularly impenetrable and mournful silence that suddenly fell, they understood the separation was definite, and silently, they withdrew.

27

Ben's departure had made little difference to Ada's life. She refused to leave her lodgings, which Harry considered a hovel. She refused to take any money from her lover.

She had sold a few paintings. She drew caricatures for some newspapers. There was quite a bit of curiosity about her, but she discouraged the snobs, the prying, the professional enthusiasts and those who speculated on new talent. She would have found it disgraceful to profit from her relationship with Harry, to become accepted into high society, make contacts or earn money. In reality, she had remained, and would always remain, a timid child who was only comfortable when completely alone. Laurence was right: Ada wasn't a woman. She had no feminine failings or virtues; she did not know how to decorate her shabby room to make it warm and welcoming, or create an attractive, peaceful atmosphere. On the contrary: the air around her seemed heavy with silent passion and, strange as it might seem, it was this, above all else, which bound Harry to her. She gave him something that, until now, had been missing in his life, but which he needed, without even realising it: deeply rooted passion, a burning within him that made the smallest of pleasures more intense, and managed to distil a wild, bitter happiness even from disappointments and sorrows.

He admired her deliberate asceticism, her disdain for the outside world, which was so unlike anything he had experienced up until now. In her, he scarcely recognised the rich, heavy blood that flowed through the veins of his family; although it was the same blood, it had the swift fluidity of an animal's blood, he thought, smiling to himself, a wild animal who had not yet been tamed.

Like Ben, she could happily go without food and sleep. She had no need of the kind of relationships, clothing or perfect surroundings that Laurence so loved.

'You live as if you're on a desert island,' he said.

'I've never lived any other way. What's the point of becoming attached to something you have to give up?'

'But why would you have to give it up, Ada?'

'I don't know. It's our destiny. Everything has always been taken away from me.'

'Well, what about me? You love me; you belong with me, don't you?'

'It's different with you. I grew up without ever seeing you, almost without knowing you, yet you belonged to me then just as you do now. I'm the kind of person who constantly fears something terrible will happen, yet I'm not afraid of losing you. You can forget me, desert me, leave me, but you'll always be mine and mine alone. I invented you, my love. You are much more than my lover. You are my creation. And that's why you belong to me, almost in spite of yourself.'

They were stretched out on the small grey-twill sofa in Ada's bedroom. On the table sat a heavy earthenware bowl of fruit, the subject of a still life that Ada had just painted. In this austere, almost bare room, Harry's few possessions seemed to have dropped in from another world: books with expensive bindings, a brown English travelling rug with silver threads, an American radio the size of a cigarette case, and the beautiful flowers that Harry sent her every day, but which were arranged in ordinary glass bottles. Everything else looked the same: the plain wooden table, a broken chair, Ben's old trunk which had made the journey from Russia to Europe; it had an arched lid with ornamental hinges and, inside, there were pictures of flowers, butterflies and birds that Ada and Ben used to decorate it when they were children.

Ada had wrapped herself in the travelling rug and was resting, her cheek against her bare arm. Both of them spoke quietly; the bedroom was cold, but the heavy blanket and warmth of their bodies against each other created a soft, almost sensual heat that nothing could equal, thought Harry, in its peaceful tranquillity. They reminisced about sleigh rides in the icy cold when, huddled beneath furs, they'd felt safe and drowsy, and the warmth had reached right to their hearts.

'When we go travelling together . . .' he said.

'Together?' Ada broke in. 'But could we do that?'

'Would you like to?'

Ada's dark eyes were shining, flames rose to her cheeks.

'No, no, it isn't possible! . . . Oh, why didn't I go to your house, your expensive house, as I'd so often dreamed of doing, *before* you were married? You would have liked me . . . You would have gone with me . . . But no, no, even then it was too late! Why weren't you like Ben, like us? Why were you born rich? Why were you tied down by furniture and paintings and books and bank accounts, by a thousand chains? But I'm also spoiled now,' she said, after a moment's silence. 'I've been tainted by the scent of happiness you breathe in this country. Give me a few more years and I'll start wishing for a set of pots and pans or a wardrobe, as if that was the greatest possible joy on earth! Even now, I already wish . . .'

'What do you wish?'

She smiled but didn't answer. He slid his arm beneath her neck.

'How shy you are, Ada! Shy and solitary, in body and soul . . .'

'You know,' she said timidly, 'it's not so strong a feeling now that spring has come, but last winter . . . There's that time of year when it gets dark so early . . . Sometimes, at four o'clock, because I'd been working since early morning and I knew I was seeing you later on, I would rest here for a while so I wouldn't look too tired and dishevelled . . . But it was the time of day when children come out of school, and I'd think, I couldn't help myself thinking about all the women rushing about in the rain, at dusk, going to collect their little girls. You can't imagine what I would have given to be in their place . . . You can't imagine,' she said again, in anguish, 'and just as I dreamed of loving you when I was a child, dreamed of my life with you, just as it is now, I imagined that, at four o'clock. I had to hurry, that I mustn't forget the jam sand-wiches for the tea or the hooded raincoat if the weather was bad. Then I'd dream of walking back home, holding my child by the hand. But I don't think such a thing is possible. God did not intend that for me. He created me to live cut off from the true life of a woman, to find my joy and my pain in different ways from other women.'

'That isn't true! You've waited for me and now I'm yours,' he said quietly, 'and if you want, we can go away together.'

She understood what he meant and started trembling.

'She knows, doesn't she?'

'She's known for a long time.'

'Oh, Harry! . . . Is she leaving you?'

'We're separating, without arguments and without tears.'

'But what about your son?'

'She doesn't wish to take my son away from me. I'll see him often and have him with me during the holidays.'

'Are you going to get a divorce?'

'Yes. And then I'll marry you.'

She pulled back in terror:

'Can you see me hosting your dinner parties, receiving your friends, listening to your aunts talk to me about painting? Can you picture me wearing one of those ridiculous little hats that look like a saucer, decorated with flowers?'

'You can still go out without a hat, if you want to,' he said, laughing. 'There's no law that says a woman must wear a hat.'

But she wasn't laughing; her lips were trembling and her eyes welled up with tears.

'I'm afraid . . . afraid of dragging you down with me . . .'

'What do you mean?' he asked softly.

She hid her face in her hands.

'I used to dream about going into your house. You would be sitting with your mother and your aunts, surrounded by them, protected by them. But I came up from behind. No one saw me. I grabbed you by your long hair – you had curls like a little girl, Harry . . .'

'Oh, have pity,' he said, smiling, 'don't drag up that terrible memory . . .'

'I would take you by the hair, like Delilah took Samson, and I'd say, "Come with me!" and you would leave everything to go with me. But where would I take you? That was what I never knew. I would wake up quivering with joy. But I know the answer now. It wasn't that I was climbing up to your level: I was dragging you down, pulling you down, by force, to mine!'

'Ada, I belonged to you before anyone else. Laurence wasn't wrong about that. She would have forgiven me an affair with a woman like her, but it is you that she cannot forgive me. It is not within our power to change what someone else has decided.'

28

It was an evening at the end of August, and Ada was alone. The divorce proceedings were about to begin. It was almost impossible to believe that life was going to change this way, that she was going to become Harry's legal wife . . . and yet . . . Hadn't everything in her life fallen upon her like lightning from above? Everything: both happiness and misfortune. God grants some people a peaceful, secure path, thought Ada, but for others an abyss awaits every step they take. From the depths of her memory, her father's words came to her, and his sad, mocking voice:

'God knows what He is doing and so He gives these unfortunate people a light, agile tread that saves them from the edge of the precipice; the storm rains down on them but they survive. He also grants them moments of great happiness, which are just as unexpected and almost as terrifying as their disasters.'

The bell rang. It couldn't be Harry; he had only just gone. She opened the door and saw Ben, the same Ben, or so it seemed, as the one who had left a few years before. He looked untouched by work or weariness or time. It had always seemed as if he was ruled by different laws to those of other mortals: disappointment made him look older; a glimmer of hope made him seem young again. He slipped into the room rather than entering it, sliding furtively through the door, as silent as a shadow. 'But of course he's just the same as ever,' Ada thought wryly. It was in exactly this way that he used to come back from one of his errands in the lower town, or from a secret fishing trip to the river, at night.

Just as she used to, Ada leapt towards him, grabbed him by the arm and shook him.

'What are you doing here?'

'I've come to say goodbye,' he replied.

'You're going away?'

'Yes.'

'Tonight?'

'Yes.'

'What have you done?'

He had gone to sit on the bed.

'There's a warrant out for me,' he said, leaning against the pillow and closing his eyes for a moment.

'Just one?' she asked.

'You've always had a great sense of humour, my girl,' he said, smiling.

She took his hand in hers.

'Well, then! You should go, get away; what are you waiting for?'

'They never arrest anyone at night. And besides, by the time it all gets going, all their complicated legal, bureaucratic, police procedures, I'll be far away . . .'

'But what have you done?' she pleaded, her voice full of fear.

He stood up and paced back and forth around the room, opening and closing the cupboards.

'What are you looking for? Money?'

He didn't reply.

'Are you hungry?' she asked.

'No. Just thirsty. I'm dying of thirst. Give me something to drink.'

She poured him a glass of water.

'Give me a drop of wine, Ada.'

'You already seem drunk!'

He wasn't listening to her. He'd found a bit of white wine and mixed it with the water. He sipped it slowly, standing up.

'No luggage?'

'No.'

'Just like before,' she murmured, 'with three shirts and a raincoat, always ready to leave, as light as the wind, a passport in your pocket . . .'

'Why do you want me to have changed?' he asked dryly. 'And what about you? The mistress of that rich Sinner, but you're still here!'

He thought for a moment, then added, 'You do know that I won't be the only one who has to leave, don't you?'

'Meaning what?'

'Meaning that someone – who is certainly not expecting it, someone who is now sleeping in his lovely French bed – would be wise to do what I'm doing, tomorrow morning or even tonight, if he doesn't want to lose everything along with me.'

'Are you mad? Have you been drinking?'

'I'm not mad and I'm not drunk. But you'll soon find out what I'm talking about.'

'Have you managed to get Harry mixed up in your dirty business, in your damned shady schemes?' she shouted.

'Absolutely.'

'Harry? But that's not possible! You and he have nothing to do with each other!'

'He and I may have nothing to do with each other, but his uncles and his company do, and there are many unpleasant, painful things in store for him as a result.'

'What are you talking about? Tell me!'

'You can read about it in the papers tomorrow!'

Ada's eyes were flashing.

'Tell me right now!' she said, leaping at him. 'Tell me, damn you!'

'The stock market crash of the Sinner firm,' he said. 'It's been kept secret until today, but tomorrow the news will break, and with all the usual consequences: legal proceedings, scandal, public outrage, et cetera.'

His long, agile hands, never at rest, traced an elegant shape in the air, a web that was as extravagant and complicated as lace; he smiled as his eyes followed its threads.

'You know, however brilliant and elaborate the scheme, it is a fragile, delicate structure that can come tumbling down with a single blow. And we've had one disaster after the other. What can you do? In the past, it was individuals who went bankrupt. But we've been dealing with insolvent governments. One after the other, they've collapsed, and every bankruptcy has been followed by some revolution or other, a change of regime or a war, and we were left high and dry with our mines flooded, our factories destroyed and our railways nationalised. What a year! I've lived through more this past twelve months than in the last twelve years. I did what I could . . .'

He stopped and looked at her.

'Yes. You've guessed right. I stopped at nothing. I wanted to save time. In deals like these, it all finally comes down to seeing how long you can hold on. You dig a hole to fill in another hole until everything caves in and the whole thing collapses . . . or you're saved by a single stroke of good luck. I've been accused of forgery.'

He shrugged his shoulders.

'I had to keep going because of my enemies and also because of the Sinners. The past six months . . . yes, it's true . . . I did forge their signatures. I had to. There were certain documents to do with assets that I had to . . . sort out a little . . . change the dates to get the creditors to wait. Everything could have been saved if we'd held our nerve and kept it quiet for a few more months. The revolutions are coming to an end; the regimes are changing. The natural resources I was counting on are still there. But you're always having to hand out bribes. That's what can become costly . . . both for me and for them. One young lad who worked for me committed suicide. You can play around with the figures and that's all right, but there's always the human element; it's inherently flawed, but you can't do without it. Every man has his petty ambitions, his pitiful little love story, his fears. One fool lost his head and killed himself; before he died, he wrote a letter to the State Prosecutor. That's how everything came out. Did the Sinners know?' he asked slowly, speaking less to Ada than to himself. 'No, of course not. Not at first, at least. And afterwards, they kept quiet because they understood how much could be gained. They were intoxicated by the idea. They rushed ahead, seeing nothing, forgetting about all the obstacles, like old horses who've been locked up in the stables for a long time,' he said with a harsh laugh. 'They hear shouting and the sound of the whip again and start running, and they run until they drop down dead. But at least I really made them run again. They had good times with me. You can't even begin to imagine what they gained, thanks to me, and especially what they might have gained! Their company was large, famous, established, but with no power, slow, uncompromising, stagnating, dying: a corpse! I'm the one who brought it back to life, make no mistake about that!'

'And Harry's uncles, those old men, listened to you?'

'Because I appealed to something within them that was even older than they were,' he said quietly.

'And Harry?'

'We fixed it so he wouldn't know anything.'

'Well, then, he's not responsible,' she cried. 'He can't be expected to answer for what you've done!'

'That will all be decided during the proceedings, my dear,' he said sarcastically.

'What proceedings?'

'But . . . there will have to be an inquiry, judges, an investigation, how should I know?'

'You mean a scandal! Is that what you wanted? A scandal?'

He didn't reply.

'You're disgusting, Ben. You are the person I mistrust and detest most in the world, the person who is most evil! There is no punishment too harsh for you. Because of you, innocent people will be prosecuted, poor people will die. An honest man will be ruined, dishonoured, and all because of you! While you, you'll disappear, calmly on your way, your hands in your pockets, your full pockets . . .'

'That's where you're wrong! I haven't got a penny.'

'Tell that to someone who might believe you,' said Ada harshly.

'I swear. Why would I lie to you? I have nothing. Do you think I was wanting to stash away pennies like some old farmer's wife from the Auvergne or Flanders when all those millions were floating around me, created by me, by the unique actions of my intelligence and cunning? Don't laugh, Ada. Just because I've been beaten doesn't mean you should refuse to admit that my intelligence, my gifts, are as brilliant as yours and equally important. What is your painting, after all? You want to make people see through your eyes, and in the same way, I too want to bend the world to my imagination, to my desires. That was what amused me, it was that, not stuffing my pockets full of money or bringing glory to the Sinners.'

He said the name with such hatred that Ada cried out. 'The truth is that you wanted to destroy Harry! Get your revenge because I left you for him. You're so proud of yourself but you're nothing but a poor jealous child! And just like the most bourgeois husband, just like any shopkeeper whose wife has cheated on him, you wanted revenge!'

'No,' he said quietly, shaking his head. 'No. The game I was playing was so exciting, I got so carried away that I even forgot about Harry . . . But the fact that he's now mixed up in this mess, well, that *is* some consolation to me. For two days now, ever since I've known that the scandal was about to break, ever since I've been shaking all over (because you know I show off for you, Ada, and you, well, you know me so well and you either don't see it or don't want to see it, so you can be tough on me, so you don't have to feel sorry for me), ever since that moment, there has been only one thought that has consoled me: the fact that, finally, Harry's fate will be the same as mine. And why shouldn't it be? We're cousins; we come from the same line; we look alike. Ah, how satisfying it will be to see our photos side by side. Harry Sinner. Ben Sinner. Tomorrow, everyone will see those photos in the morning papers, and no one will be fooled, no one. They'll be saying: "Two dirty foreigners, two filthy immigrants. Brothers, without a doubt . . . Look at them: they have the same scheming eyes, the same greedy mouth. They're so ugly. Prison is the only place for those two!"'

He saw she had turned white.

'But you know, I don't really want him to go to prison that much,' he said, leaning towards her. 'You can warn him and let him do what I'm doing. Tell him to get away, to disappear. He won't have a penny, you realise that? . . . The Sinners' business will collapse. He can go from country to country, buying and selling rubbish, trafficking in foreign currency, become a travelling salesman, a broker who trades in cheap fabric or contraband munitions, depending on what his clients want or need, and in ten years, we'll see if anyone, even a woman in love, even you, Ada, can tell the difference between him and me.'

'Never. That's impossible. He'll never be like you, never!'

'No, he won't. He'd drown in places where I would float.'

They heard the clock strike four. Ben shivered.

'I'm going now.'

'Yes, go on, please,' said Ada, trembling, pale, her eyes burning, 'because ... I'm afraid of myself ... I want to kill you ...'

'Ada, come with me.'

'You are mad! Now I'm sure of it. You're mad!'

'Ada, he's not right for you and you're not right for him. *I* know you; I'm almost a brother to you. Come with me. Who is *he*? He's nearly a stranger to you! Come with me!'

He was no longer overexcited; the unnatural fever that had been sustaining him had abated. He spoke quietly, simply, without looking at her, without moving towards her.

'You're thinking you'll go with *him* if he leaves. But he won't leave; he'll stay, his head bowed. He'll bear the punishment that he doesn't deserve. He won't have the courage to give up everything, to get away, like I'm doing. I may have more happiness and more misfortune in store, but for him, life will be over. He'll be eaten up by shame, by futile regrets. He'll wait for the scandal to break. Then he'll wait for the trial, then he'll wait for people to forget. But they won't forget, not until after he's dead. But if you come with me ...'

'And you just said how similar you both were!' she interrupted, furious.

'Yes: the ways dogs and wolves are similar,' he said, shrugging his shoulders. 'Ada! Do you imagine for a moment that he'll forgive you?'

'Forgive *me*? I haven't done anything!'

'You forced him back amongst us, the Jewish scum, the opportunists, the immigrants, the foreigners ... What else could he be after this? He had friends, a family, a fortune, a French wife! Can you imagine the contrast? What is scandal or dishonour to me? I've never been respected! What does going into exile mean to me? I have no real home. But to him ... And you think he'll forgive you for that?'

All she could do was whisper, her voice faltering, 'You are disgusting! Go to hell! I wish you were dead! I hope you die alone!'

The ferocious curses that came from her mouth frightened even her. She fell silent.

'Come with me!' he said again. 'Will you, Ada?'

Suddenly he was speaking in an almost childlike voice, like when they were young, when he would call out to her beneath the open windows to come with him, at night, to the river's edge. And, just like back then, she replied, 'No. Go alone,' opening the door for him to leave.

He leaned forward and kissed Ada's hand. Then he went calmly down the stairs, walked out of the house and disappeared.

29

Ada ran down the stairs after him. At first she had thought of rushing over to Harry's, but she knew he couldn't be persuaded to flee. He wouldn't abandon his uncles or the business when they were threatened by scandal. How could he run away? He was still held there by so many family ties. No, it was pointless trying to find him. Besides, she felt sorry for him. It was nearly five o'clock in the morning. Let him have one more peaceful night's sleep. She was afraid of him too. Ben was right: it was all her fault. How could he ever forgive her? She had dragged him far away from his family, into her own dark and tangled woods. No, she wouldn't go to Harry's house. But whom could she turn to? Whom could she beg for help? She had no one in the world except Aunt Raissa and Madame Mimi. Aunt Raissa had come back to France when Lilla had abandoned her prince, running off with the leading court musician.

Ada walked up the staircase that, a few years before, she had fled down, her cheeks still burning from the slap she'd received, to throw herself into Ben's arms. On the first floor, there was an empty little alcove made of painted wood, and she remembered how she had stopped there for a moment before rushing away and running into the street. And now she was hurrying to Aunt Raissa to ask for help!

When she remembered this, she clung on to the memory for a moment and managed to give shape to an idea that was her only bitter consolation: 'If you've forgotten that, you'll also forget about Ben, and Harry.'

She'd reached the door; she rang the bell and knocked several times. Aunt Raissa finally appeared; she was still slim and agile, but her red hair had turned white and her lively, harsh expression had given way to a look of defiant and false resignation, as if she were thinking, 'Oh, I won't make the same mistake again. I know now, you don't have to tell me: it's all over for me; the bets were placed long ago, the cards dealt out, and I can only watch other people play without playing myself, happy that I'm still allowed even to be here.'

'What is it now?' she shouted, looking at Ada.

'I've just seen Ben,' she said, and her voice seemed extraordinarily calm and distant to her, detached, like the echo of someone else who had spoken her despairing words in the most self-controlled way, just to mock her. 'Ben has gone away. He was going to be arrested tonight.'

Aunt Raissa said nothing, but her cheeks and forehead turned red and blotchy, as always happened when she felt any real emotion. She never cried, which was one good thing. It was comforting to hear her say in the sullen voice that was just as it had always been, 'Come in or go out. Don't leave me standing here in a draught.'

Ada followed her inside. There were piles of material, pins and patterns all over the little sitting room, as always. Aunt Raissa automatically picked up and folded the fashion photos that covered the table. Then suddenly, she stopped, and with a surprised, weak gesture, covered her cheeks and forehead with her hands.

'It's hard at my age.'

'I know, Aunt Raissa,' Ada said, with pity.

It hadn't occurred to them to switch on the lamp; the dawn

light lit up the grey canvas tailor's dummy that stood in the corner of the room. The two women sat on the settee in silence for a moment.

'How was he?' asked Aunt Raissa.

Ada shrugged her shoulders.

'The same as ever.'

'Yes, even on the gallows he'd be the same as ever, full of hope. What did he want from you? You've separated.'

Ada didn't reply.

'Are you going with him?'

'No.'

'You're wrong. The scandal will come out and land on you too, because you're his wife and you have the same name. Whether you like it or not, you're tied to each other. You should have gone with him. What will happen to you here? Your lover will leave you. He won't forgive you for getting him mixed up in a scandal.'

'Where is Madame Mimi?' Ada asked, her voice shaking.

Madame Mimi was her last hope: unlike Ben and Aunt Raissa, she wouldn't tell her she had betrayed and ruined Harry.

Aunt Raissa pointed to the next room.

'Go to her. She's sleeping. She won't have heard you come in; she sleeps like a log. I never even close my eyes at night, not me. But she doesn't have, has never had children, the lucky thing, so she can sleep!'

Ada went into the little back bedroom that was Madame Mimi's. To her surprise, she found the old woman out of bed; she was wearing a red silk shawl with fringes and sitting at a little table with a lamp on it, her playing cards spread out in front of her. She raised her eyes and looked straight at Ada.

'Come in,' she said softly. 'I heard what you said, you poor thing. How alone and in despair you must be feeling to make you come back here!'

For the first time, Ada couldn't hold back her tears. She threw herself down into a chair and repeated everything Ben had said. Her voice was low and broken.

'What should I do, Madame Mimi?' she murmured.

'Nothing. Wait.'

'But that's impossible!' she cried, in anguish.

A smile flickered across the old woman's face.

'Ah, that's just like you, just like all of you. You fight until the very end.'

'You know as well as I do,' said Ada in a cold, distant voice that rang in her ears as if it belonged to some stranger, 'you know as well as I do that only his wife, only that French family can save him.'

'If they want to, Ada.'

'If they don't want to, then he'll be mine and mine alone . . .'

But Ben's words and Aunt Raissa's came flooding back.

'Whatever happens, I've lost him,' she said.

She had hoped for some advice from the two old women, but she now understood that nothing had changed: she had always been alone, and she would always be alone, listening only to herself, to a sort of hopeless, wise twin who was hidden deep within her.

'It's true, isn't it?' she said out loud, more to herself than to Madame Mimi. 'It's true that I have nothing to complain about, in the end. After all, if anyone had told me back then, in the Ukraine, that one day Harry Sinner would leave his wife and child for me . . .

'For me . . .' she said again.

'How you demean yourself! And you get such pleasure from doing it, such proud satisfaction . . .'

'Oh, Madame Mimi!' she begged as if she were a child. 'Who can give me the courage I need? . . . It's the only thing that can save him. I have to make his wife think that I've gone away with Ben; I have to make Harry believe it! She'll go back to him then, she loves him; she couldn't possibly allow such scandal and dishonour ... They have a child. Alone or with me, Harry is nothing. But with her and her powerful family to support him, he could be saved.'

'And what about you?'

'I'll come back here. Or I'll go away somewhere. It hardly matters ... It's so easy to disappear in this city when no one cares about you. He won't come looking for me. That's the thing I find most painful. He loves me, but he won't come looking for me. It's like when you truly want to kill yourself and someone wrenches the gun away from you: you don't put up a fight because, deep down, you're afraid of death. And to Harry, I'm that wrench, a second chance to live, or death,' she said, more quietly.

Madame Mimi nodded.

'Yes, they could come to an arrangement. The case against him could be withdrawn. With a respectable family around him, a French name to back up his own, yes, I think that would be the best thing for Harry ... I said for Harry, but for you ...'

Ada didn't reply. She had thrown herself down on the bed, exhausted. Madame Mimi looked at her, went and got a blanket and covered her with it. Then she sat down again. She had that visible impassiveness that comes with old age and which, though it seems uncaring, gives comfort without a word being spoken or a tear being shed: she was living proof of forgetfulness and the end of all things. Ada kept her eyes closed, but she wasn't asleep; she was thinking.

30

When Harry left Ada that same evening, he realised it wasn't late, so he could spend an hour with some friends who lived in the outskirts of Paris. They had been inviting him to come for some time. He'd had to turn down the dinner invitation but the party afterwards wouldn't finish until four or five in the morning. He could be there by midnight. He set off.

He went into the house. It was a warm night and the servants told him everyone was in the garden. He didn't wish to be announced and replied that he would find his hosts himself. A floodlight on the terrace lit up the small dance floor, but the grounds behind were dark.

He walked beneath the trees, hoping it would be cooler there. A few women and two men were sitting apart from the others. They were talking excitedly. Harry couldn't hear what they were saying. He walked on quietly: he had the silent step of all the Sinners. His friends didn't see him until he was quite close to them. One of them said 'Hem!' quite loudly, as you do when you want to warn indiscreet gossips. Everyone stopped talking.

Harry was not unduly bothered when he realised they were talking about him: he knew very well that his close friends were aware of his separation from Laurence and his affair with Ada. Their curiosity did not surprise him. He feared neither their judgment nor their harshness when the moment came to announce his second marriage: he lived in the world of the rich bourgeoisie where divorce and adultery were so common they shocked no one. He was even prepared for whispered jokes and sly allusions from one of the women who was there; nearly all of them had sought his 'attentions', both before and after his marriage. It was their silence that surprised him. Then one of the men called out in that artificially lively and ringing tone of voice used when you want to disguise your secret thoughts.

'Where the devil have you been hiding? We were just talking about you. No one ever sees you any more.'

'That,' thought Harry, 'is in case I hear someone say my name as I walk up to them.'

He felt mildly irritated. What did they want of him? Why couldn't they leave him be? He stopped himself, thinking it was absurd to attach such importance to malicious gossip. But, in spite of himself, his voice sounded hesitant and upset as he replied, 'Yes. I've had so much to do . . .'

Once again, silence. Every one of his words met with an attention and hostility that was barely perceptible, yet noticeable nevertheless. And, after he spoke, after making an effort to say something carefully chosen to be insignificant, the silence lasted a few seconds longer. A few seconds too long . . . like when you're waiting for a stone to hit the bottom of a ravine in order to measure its depth. He felt as if he were separated from the others by an ever-growing abyss. Then everyone started talking and laughing at the same time.

'Got lots of work on these days?' someone asked.

Harry remembered that he hadn't been seen anywhere since Laurence had left, not even in June when the members of their social circle saw each other ten times a day in ten different places. He hastened to assure his friends that he had, in fact, been very busy at work.

'You're lucky,' said the man who had first spoken to him. 'I would just as soon close down my offices and go away for six months: things couldn't be any worse.'

One of the women asked how Laurence was in a tone of voice that wasn't nasty or awkward, but the way you ask any old question in order not to ask something else, something more embarrassing.

His reply was curt and evasive. One of the couples walked away, followed by another. The two women who remained were smoking their cigarettes without saying a word.

'It's rather cool out here,' said Harry.

They seemed happy for the excuse he purposely gave them, for he could tell that they too wanted to get away from him.

'Yes, it is, isn't it?' they cried. 'It must be late. That wind coming from the lake isn't very nice.'

They stood up, smiled at him and disappeared. He remained seated where he was, watching the light that shone dimly over the lake.

With his head lowered, his thin hands clasped around his knees, and his long, delicate neck tilted to one side, he resembled a bird alone on its perch amid other birds from a different species whom he watches from a distance without daring to approach. That image came to mind in spite of himself, and remained with him from then on. He stood up, making an effort to be cheerful and proud. After all, what had he done that should make him feel guilty like this?

'Nothing,' he thought forcefully, 'nothing. My wife and I separated on good terms, and besides, my personal life is nobody's business. What's wrong with everybody tonight?'

He tried to reassure himself. On a number of occasions in the past he had surprised himself by how vulnerable he felt. He reacted so strongly to the slightest hint of blame or coldness.

'Well, I don't give a damn about these people,' he murmured brutally. 'I don't give a damn!'

He felt cold, yet his forehead was covered in perspiration. Nervously he wrung his hands.

'Something terrible has happened,' he thought. 'Something I know nothing about. But *they* all know!'

His immediate thought was of the bank. He hadn't been there in over a week. For two years he had lived with a vague yet over-powering sense of foreboding, but – and this was what was so strange – not only did this state of fear, of muffled panic, not surprise him, it was as if he recognised it, just as a man returning to the seaside home of his childhood tastes the bitterness of the ocean on his lips even before he hears it. Instinctively, without knowing exactly what it was that he feared, he had employed all the defensive reflexes that make it possible to deal with anxiety. He knew which thoughts were acceptable and which had to be dismissed; he knew how to prepare his mind to be watchful in order to cover up the very thing that he would nevertheless have to admit one day and which was impossible to prevent. He had learned how to bear insomnia, apprehension and that sudden pounding of his heart every time the telephone rang unexpect-edly, every time the doorbell rang. Learned? No! He had always known these things.

Women in pink dresses walked by beneath the trees; the men were laughing, the little burning ends of their cigars lighting up their peaceful, happy faces. They were his friends; he had never seen any difference between him and them. He now wondered if he hadn't actually been mistaken, if they really understood him and how they would treat him if something terrible happened to him.

For he knew that something terrible had happened. He could sense it; he could feel it in the air, just as animals can smell a storm getting closer . . . It was all coming back to him: that icy hand clutching at his heart, the inability to breathe followed by the gasping for air, the thirst, the overwhelming sadness. Nothing seemed surprising to him: not his silent resignation, nor his invincible hope. ('It will take a lot of courage, a lot of work. Who else in this world can pride themselves on having as much or more courage and ability to work than me? And besides, it will pass. Everything has already happened, I don't know where or when, but I have already lost everything and found it again. None of it is of any real importance. Death itself is of no real importance.') He acknowledged all his fantasies, all his anguish. And, every now and again, he awoke as if from a dream and thought, 'But what has actually happened? These people have been cold towards me, that's all. Why is that so unusual? At least two of those women sent me invitations and I cancelled at the last minute, that's all, that's enough; and the man is a fool! ... After all, I know I'm not guilty of anything. No, I haven't done anything! I'm innocent!'

But had he ever felt that blessed certainty of being innocent, of being forgiven, of being loved? No! He had been born feeling guilty of a crime he had not committed, knowing that no one would intervene for him, no one would save him, that he would be alone with a fearsome god.

Suddenly, he could no longer bear his solitude. He stood up and joined the groups of people passing by. He listened to the women laughing; he walked to the lake, then went back to the house. Very few people were left. He wandered through the half empty reception rooms. He asked for his car. As he was crossing the terrace, he heard another voice behind him whisper, 'Harry Sinner ...'

He shivered. Who had spoken his name? He turned around, waited. But no one had called him. Someone was just talking about him. Everyone was talking about him tonight. He felt lost.

In his car, he sat up, calm and straight, but gradually his arms drooped, he lowered his head and hunched his shoulders. Thin and frail, rubbing his beautiful hands together, he swayed gently in the darkness, just as so many moneychangers standing behind their counters, just as countless rabbis bent over their books, just as a multitude of immigrants standing on the bridges of innumberable boats had done before him. And, like them, he felt like an outsider, lost and alone.

31

How easy it is to disappear for a girl like Ada. She paid for the furnished room, packed her books into Ben's little trunk, put some clothes into a suitcase, took down the pictures from the walls, folded the soft, warm blanket Harry had given her into an old hat box and left.

'Aren't you going to give me a forwarding address?' the concierge had asked. 'If the gentleman, you know who I mean, if he asks for you, what am I supposed to say?'

'Say that I went away with my husband.'

'Really?'

The concierge looked at her with pity. Presumably the police had already questioned her about Ben.

'If he really wanted to find me,' Ada thought, 'the Immigration Office or the Prefect of Police could give him information, but he'll think I've gone far away, to another country. He can't leave France now to come and find me, and it's better that way. It's definitely better that way.'

She had gone into a post office and written a note to Harry:

'I'm going with Ben. This is goodbye.'

What else could she say? Her heart was as heavy and cold as stone, even her mind, normally so quick and lively, seemed inert and dull, or as if numbed by the cold. If only she could believe she would remain like that, the future might seem bearable, but she knew very well that she would wake up one day and realise exactly what she had lost.

For two days, she had walked back and forth past Laurence's house. At first, she thought she would go to her, explain the situation as it was, make her understand that she was pretending to leave Harry, that she was sacrificing herself for Harry. She felt a rather base, though irrefutable, pleasure – the kind of pleasure you feel watching a play at the theatre – in imagining Laurence's confusion, astonishment and admiration. For Laurence would have admired her . . . She walked along the scorching street (it was the end of August, and the days were unbearably hot) and looked up at the high, large windows with envy. How big and cool the rooms must be behind their closed shutters! She would be ushered in to see Laurence. 'Take him back,' she would say. 'I've got what I wanted. I won't ask for anything more. I do not wish him to lose everything because of me.' She hated herself for bringing pride into her love; was pride really so deeply engrained in her heart, the 'hardened heart' that the Scriptures mention? And could she rid herself of it any more than she could rid herself of her own blood?

She was afraid that Laurence might have left Paris at this time of year, when all the windows in the rich neighbourhoods are locked and the apartments empty. But she had made enquiries: all of the Delarchers were still in the city, and this seemed a sign of hope to Ada. Not all the ties between Harry and his wife had been broken. Laurence still cared about Harry; she didn't want to leave him. 'Perhaps she made up some excuse to remain in Paris?' thought Ada. A savage, almost maternal sadness tore through her when she imagined Harry feeling so abandoned, so alone; at such moments, she believed she might actually have the courage to go into Laurence's house and drag her to Harry's door. But she didn't dare.

Forty-eight hours had already passed as if in a dark, terrifying dream.

'I am leaving to go with my husband who has been deported from France,' she wrote to Laurence. 'You must understand that I will never return and that you can both forget me . . .'

But she stopped. She tore up the letter. It was essential that she hear from Laurence's own lips that she would go back to her husband and, more importantly, that the elderly Delarcher would not abandon his son-in-law . . . And this was Ada's secret hope. She would do anything in the world to save Harry. But what if that wasn't possible?

At other times, she thought, 'I'll pretend to disappear. Everything will get sorted out, and then . . .' But the danger was too great, too pressing: it could only be averted by completely sacrificing any possibility of happiness.

'If I do that, God will punish me,' she thought.

She would stop and look, from a distance, at the Catholic churches with their rows of lit candles, visible through the doors left open on such hot days. But it was the same as looking at Laurence's house: all of that was a different world, a world she was not allowed to enter. She kept walking, endlessly walking. She was aching with thirst; she stopped for a few moments in a little square in the neighbourhood where Laurence lived: cool water flowed from a fountain. She wet her hands and face, then set off again.

Finally, on the evening of the second day, she saw Laurence coming out of her house. She had only seen her a few times before; up until now, she had thought of her without attributing to her any truly human characteristics: she was Harry's wife. She was part of that brilliant circle who, ever since she and Harry were born, had come between them, dazzling her, as cold and blurred as the stars in the sky. Now she truly saw her: she was a young, beautiful woman, but neither her youth nor her beauty had that other-worldly essence that Ada had imagined. She was not a goddess: she was a blonde whose complexion would quickly lose its bloom, and which was reddened by the heat. Ada was overwhelmed by fear and a physical sensation of jealousy that she had never felt before: fear because it occurred to her that Laurence might not have the power she attributed to her, and with this thought, all her ideas suddenly seemed flawed, all her hopes were lifted up and dashed, like wisps of straw carried off in a whirlwind. She doubted the superiority, the omnipotence of the French family. She had believed that all she had to do was return Harry to the Delarchers in order to save him, but was that really true? Weren't there other powerful people she could go to for help? This was how her ancestors had spent their lives on earth: desperately seeking ever more influential, more highly placed protectors, but never finding them, constantly anxious about the ones they had found – these men who had once had God as their master but had forsaken Him. And to feel the great Laurence so close to her, so similar to an ordinary woman, she finally understood simple feminine jealousy: she could imagine Harry reconciled with his wife, which meant sharing her room, her bed, caressing her. Fierce loathing filled her heart.

'Finally I can see Harry as the same as me,' she thought, 'truly the same as me, brought up on the same bitter bread, and I'm hesitating! I want to send him back to his wife, his child, his Canalettos in the dining room I hardly dare enter, back to his expensive leather books bearing the arms of French kings, back to everything that makes him a stranger to me? Never! Never!'

She was crying. Passers-by looked at her, but she had cried far more often in the streets, amid a crowd, than she ever had in private, behind closed shutters and drawn curtains; it wasn't the first time. She wasn't ashamed of her tears: she knew that no one really cared, that she could sob as much as she liked, collapsed on a bench, without causing any reaction other than a policeman shrugging his shoulders and saying, 'Come, come . . . you mustn't get so upset. Come on, my girl . . .'

She cried for a long time beneath the trees on the wide avenue. Her hair was dishevelled and her cheek bruised by the iron bars of the gate she'd been leaning on; only one child stopped and looked at her with serious, kindly pity. She smiled at him through her tears.

'Is your little boy sick?' he got up the courage to ask her.

She shook her head. He was a young boy who was quite dirty, but his fat cheeks were rosy and soft. He walked over to her and stroked Ada's knees with his dirty hands.

'Do you have a child?'

'Yes,' she replied.

She had been afraid to ask herself that very question, but now that she had answered this strange little boy, she felt a sense of peace again. She dried her eyes.

Now that she had stopped crying, in the eyes of the child she turned back into a frightening and incomprehensible adult, like all grown-ups. He took a step away, and even though she called out to him, he didn't move forward; he just continued staring at her with mistrust and fear. Ada felt as if her last friend had abandoned her. She stood up and went back to stand in front of Laurence's house. It was nearly eight o'clock; the young woman had been wearing day clothes and would surely be coming home for dinner. She waited for a long time and finally saw Laurence. She had sensed her, even before recognising her, because of a strange, sudden pain in her heart. She walked quickly towards Laurence.

Laurence stopped; she started with a slight gesture of fear mixed with revulsion, thought Ada. Ada looked at her now without hatred, but with deep concentration, as if she were studying a model's face.

'I must guess what she has truly decided to do by watching her eyes and not by what she says,' Ada thought, 'and then plan my life according to what I read in her expression.'

'I'm going away in an hour,' she said.

'Oh?' said Laurence, moving to one side as if trying to avoid her. But her movement was hesitant, slow and half-hearted, as when you dream you are struggling in deep water, in quicksand, in murky lakes that overwhelm you and carry you away.

'I will never come back, Madame. I'll never see Harry again.'

'Please leave.'

Suddenly, Ada grabbed the stunned Laurence by the hand.

'Listen to me,' she said, 'you are the only one who will know the truth. Harry thinks I've gone to be with my husband. It's not true. I'm still here in Paris. I could choose either to go away or stay near him and try to get him back. But I swear to you that I will never go near him again, never remind him I even exist; I won't speak to him or write to him, if you think that would save him.'

Laurence said nothing, but she didn't try to leave. She too was concentrating on watching Ada's face, hoping, no doubt, to read the thoughts of this strange foreigner.

'Do you want to help him?'

Laurence nodded; making a scene right there in the street seemed to cause her pain, thought Ada, as if some unbearable vulgarity had been added to her resentment and suffering.

'Poor Harry . . .' she suddenly thought. 'Unhappy with her, unhappy with me, caught between two burning fires, between two races, what will become of him?'

'Are you in a position to help him?'

'I'm not,' she replied quietly, 'but my father is.'

'Yes, that's what I thought. Would he be willing to do it?'

'Yes, if we agree not to get divorced. Did Harry? . . .' She stopped, blushing sadly. 'Did Harry try to find you?'

'No.'

They fell silent.

'Do you think that everything could be saved, Madame,' Ada asked once more, 'and that things would return to the way they were before, as if I'd never existed?'

Both women, overwhelmed by fear and hatred, looked at each other and said nothing. Ada didn't move; she felt that by walking away from Laurence, she was losing Harry, and that everything truly would be as if he had never existed.

'Just like in fairy tales,' she thought in astonishment, 'when you find yourself standing in front of a cracked mirror or a light that's switched off, and the spell is broken.'

Yes, this woman, this Laurence, was a link between her and Harry, the only living link. One word, one step, and it would all be over. She had rewound her life once more; she was back to where she had started. With difficulty, she let go of Laurence. She didn't run: she walked slowly away, head down. But her heart, her heart that never gave up hope, began to quiver, whispering from within her: 'I lost him before and then found him. Perhaps that will happen again?'

No! She had to sacrifice him once and for all. She forced herself to overcome her stubborn desire for happiness and the belief that lived inside her, that absurd, incomprehensible belief, that Harry was truly destined to be hers.

She walked on with difficulty, clutching the gates along the avenue, her lips burning, her legs leaden and painful. But she shed no tears.

32

Ada very rarely received any post. So when an official letter addressed to her arrived at her house, she experienced a moment of blind hope. But it wasn't Harry's handwriting. It was only a deportation order, with a period of one week allowed for the necessary formalities to be completed. Ben was nowhere to be found. Perhaps they weren't looking for him very hard: ever since Delarcher had taken his son-in-law's affairs in hand, the gossip surrounding the 'scandal of a group of international financiers', as it was called, had died down, and as Ben was the principal figure in a trial that everyone wished to avoid at all costs, it was hoped that he might not be in France. But just as the waves carry seaweed and shells down into the sea along with the corpse of a drowned man, so provident justice swept away those close to the famous Ben Sinner, forcing his family, his mother and his wife into exile.

All this happened with the greatest possible discretion: the newspapers were not alerted; Harry was told nothing. His business continued as businesses do in such circumstances. After a long article in the evening paper, no further information had appeared until several days had passed, and then only on the second page, in smaller print; after that, the story had disappeared, turning up as a short paragraph among minor news items before vanishing entirely. Only a few small local rags printed articles about it again, just as a starving dog grabs the remains of a meal that others have left behind, gnawing in vain at a bone. There were a few vague threats, promises of details to come, but then political events of great importance occurred and everything went quiet.

After such a scare, the established business resumed its calm, dignified attitude, like a sick man who has revealed certain things about his youth, his shameful past and vile love affairs while delirious, and then wakes up without any memory of what he said during the night. (And even if he does eventually remember, he isn't worried: only the professionals around him heard, the doctors and nurses; no one would find out anything.)

When the deportation order arrived, Aunt Raissa rushed to find Ada, begging her to go to Harry, to save them. Where would she go? What country would have her? How would she earn a living?

Then she received a mysterious telegram and calmed down. Ada realised she had been in touch with Ben. A new boutique would soon be opening in a South American country far away, 'Little Paris' or 'French Fashion', and the spirited, hard Aunt Raissa, her hair now dyed a youthful red colour, would recover her former strength and begin a new life. She was already making plans, deciding which patterns to take with her, more or less illegally, while still trying to have the decree forcing her to leave repealed.

That evening, one by one, all of Aunt Raissa's friends arrived, all the immigrants she had known in Paris. They formed an extraordinary tableau of withered faces, heavy bodies, dull eyes. There were Jews from Odessa and Kiev, former ladies-in-waiting to the Empress, ladies of the court who had shone for a time after their exile but who were now living on black bread, as they put it. There were the wives and widows of corrupt financiers who had either died, gone on the run or were in prison. To all the women, the announcement of a deportation of one of their own had a precise, sinister meaning. It meant that they too, sooner or later, could fall prey to the same decree; they too, one fine day, might have to leave their sordid little furnished room, the Parisian street that consoled all of them with its bustle, cheerfulness, clear skies and polite passers-by, only to wait endlessly at the consulates for a passport they'd been promised but which never arrived, then to leave in search of a precarious means of existence. They avoided showing their faces during the day, thinking there were spies and policemen everywhere; in the evening, they were braver. They climbed the stairs to Aunt Raissa's door, sat in a circle around the lamp and stared at the open trunk in the middle of the room, an ominous symbol. Whenever they heard a noise – the concierge's footsteps on the stairs, someone knocking at a door, the telephone ringing – they picked up their skirts and ran, just as chickens scurry in all directions when one of them is chased and caught.

Speaking softly, they exchanged addresses and advice:

'I know the wife of the chief of police quite well . . .'

'Well, my lodger has a daughter who's a secretary in the Home Office . . .'

With their faded hair, sad eyes, hunched shoulders beneath Russian shawls, threadbare black dresses, small hands that were still pretty but had broken nails from doing menial work, they leaned in towards Aunt Raissa's lamp, and the smoke from their endless cigarettes wafted around them. Ada found them strangely fascinating. In their soft, melodic voices, they compared the advantages of different countries:

'My husband wrote to me to say that Venezuela . . .'

'Ah, my dear, don't talk to me about that place . . . They say that Brazil . . .'

'But the climate, the snakes . . .'

'I've heard there are still some places left for immigrants in Canada . . .'

Then, gradually, because they were elderly for the most part
– the young people had other problems and didn't go to Aunt
Raissa's – and because even old age has its brighter side, a carefree, frivolous and melancholy way of evading the truth, of closing
its eyes and forgetting the future, even the most pressing, the most
threatening of futures, they started talking about recipes and
dresses, and their senile chatter, interspersed with little bursts of
laughter and brief affected cries, covered up the sighs that each
of them occasionally heaved. In general, they didn't feel as sorry
for Ada as they did for her aunt:

'You're young, my girl. At your age . . . And besides, if you
wanted to . . .'

For Aunt Raissa told everyone, in great detail, with a strange
mixture of admiration and resentment, all about Ada's affair. And
Ada, gloomy and silent, sat and listened, her head bowed.

She calculated the distance between herself and these women
by the feeling of shame she felt. Through her relationship with
Harry, and for her sins, she had become sophisticated. The way
they made a show of their woes, their resignation to being
outsiders, was this her fate as well? Anywhere she went with
Aunt Raissa, she would find herself surrounded once more by
these powdered faces that looked like hastily patched-up ruins,
women who had nothing left in this world, no husbands, no children, no homes. Everything she had scorned, she now clung on
to in despair, just as she was about to lose it. She had so often
mocked Harry: she would say that he was not the owner but the
slave of his wealth:

'You belong to your precious Nankin cups,' she used to say, 'to
your jade collections, to your books . . .'

How wonderful it would be, she now thought, to belong to an
object, or a person, or a collection of traditions, conventions and
customs. To own things, to fit in, what did that matter? But to
have bonds that were complex and intricate, or solid and heavy,

and not to remain, like these women, like she herself, a being with no roots, carried along by the wind . . .

In the afternoon, when they brought tea in from the kitchen in a collection of mismatched cups and sugar on a saucer (the sugar bowl had been broken), Ada went into the other room. She stretched out on the settee, beneath Harry's blanket, the only precious thing she owned. It was at this hour that Harry's face, an image she had bravely fought off all day long, came back to her and took hold of her. She thanked God, in spite of everything. She had retained the power she'd had as a child to fantasise, to imagine scenes that were closer, more vivid to her than reality. For over a week, she hadn't touched a paintbrush or canvas: it was just too difficult. It was impossible to work with the knowledge that she couldn't show her painting to Harry, couldn't hear his criticisms or his praise. But this slow, unyielding, involuntary working of her mind, this was her treasure. She conjured up Harry, she was with him again; she spoke to him. The women's voices rose and fell; here on this street in Paris, they miraculously managed to carry her back to the distant past. Wasn't that Ben she could hear, practising his Hebrew in the next room? Wasn't she that little girl whose thick hair fell over her eyes as she burned with a desire to sleep, always waiting, always hoping? She hid her face in her hands. No one saw her crying. All those women had shed so many tears that they didn't notice them any more than they noticed the rain falling in autumn.

'These are my people,' thought Ada, 'my family.'

Nevertheless, on the day that her resident's permit to live in France expired, Ada said goodbye to her aunt, hugged a silent, tearful Madame Mimi, and, abandoning Ben, her memory of him and her memory of Harry, abandoning hope, she left, all alone. She had been granted a visa to live in a small country in Eastern Europe.

33

The child would soon be born. The birth would take place in March, in a small town in Eastern Europe, in a hotel room above the marketplace. Ada couldn't get a bed in a hospital because civil war had broken out a few days earlier – a continual occurrence in the country – accompanied by a series of strikes and retaliations: the hospitals were all full. They might be able to find room for their own citizens, she'd been told, but not for foreigners.

Ada had acquiesced. She was used to it. She was not completely without resources, however: ten years spent in Paris provides valuable experience. She had found a job as a sales assistant in a bazaar on the main street. She modelled fashionable 'Parisian hats' over her black hair, which she had grown back into the style she had worn in the past. The local women found them tempting and bought little saucer-shaped hats decorated with flowers, or turbans swathed with polka-dot netting which they perched high on their red or blonde hair. Whenever she was weary of all the grey and darkness around her, Ada took pleasure in studying their dazzling hair, the colour of wheat and gold. Winter was long: the light shimmered for a few hours over the snow, then turned blood-red, piercing the fog above the river like an arrow before disappearing. By the time Ada came out of the shop, there was nothing but darkness all around. It wasn't like night in Paris, where street lamps and shop signs lit up the dark: here there were icy shadows, a cruel, black sky where high rooftops covered in snow stood out in sharp detail. The ditches on both sides of the street were so deep that she was afraid of falling at every step, so she walked with great difficulty, teeth clenched, head down; it never even occurred to her to look up at the cold, brilliant stars, closer and brighter here than in Paris.

On Sundays, she stayed at home and painted all day long; she felt happy then, because the only effort she had to make was to choose which shade of silvery white best suited her secret desire, or to look at the women's faces she'd seen during the day, the women with their long blonde hair. When the light faded, she remembered that her condition required her to go for a walk, to get some fresh air, so she would make her way slowly downstairs and head for the river that divided the town into two parts; in some places, people were skating. An open space was cordoned off by strings of lights and you could see the quick, light silhouettes gliding across the ice. A little orchestra was playing a noisy, jarring fanfare, but to Ada, it sounded softer; the wind dispersed the sounds that were too harsh and the blaring of the brass instruments. Some sleighs passed by, their lamps casting a yellowish glow that danced on the ice; the skaters who came out of the circle also pinned little paper lanterns on to their jackets, so each of their gliding movements created a short, luminous streak of light.

Sometimes a man would see Ada standing there; he would go up to her, attracted by the black hair fluttering across her pale face, but as soon as he saw she was pregnant, he would walk away without a word. She could stand there as long as she pleased and think back to last year, and the year before . . . think, remember, regret, cry . . . until the iron bar on the bridge froze her fingers and they felt numb and painful. She went back home, and her neighbour brought her a modest meal from a nearby restaurant.

The woman was also an immigrant; she had been rejected first by America, then by Germany. She had two sons in one country in Europe and a daughter in another; her husband was imprisoned in a concentration camp. Such circumstances formed a special class of people that existed beyond caste and race, a world apart, where helping each other was the only moral code. Ada, who earned a good living and had few needs, sometimes gave some money or an old dress to her neighbour, who in turn helped Ada with chores she found difficult to do. It was understood, almost without any discussion, through a sort of mutual understanding, that when the child was born, it would be this woman – Rose Liebig – who would look after him while Ada continued to work.

The unrest broke out a few days before the birth: at dawn, they saw soldiers charging through the empty marketplace. When they had gone, Ada leaned out of the open window and saw a hotchpotch of objects rolling about in the snow: empty baskets, tarpaulins, bread, strings of onions; some farmers' wives had arrived during the night with their wares but had fled. They heard gunfire for several hours, then everything went quiet. The women who had run away came back with their donkeys and baskets; the older ones were crying while the youngsters laughed. Lying in her bed, Ada could hear the shouting from the market again. She didn't have the strength to get up; terrified, she imagined being rushed to hospital in a car with broken suspension, over bumpy roads. She was almost relieved when told there was no space for her anywhere.

They would manage as best they could, said Rose Liebig. The room was warm, the swaddling clothes and cradle were all ready, and they weren't short of medical assistance: the hotel was full of refugees from central Europe, the majority of whom were medical students and midwives. Ada didn't know anyone, or so she thought, but everyone knew about her condition, and she was more fussed over and spoiled that day than she'd been in all her life: they brought her apples, cushions for her and the baby, Viennese pastries, honey-covered nuts that were a Jewish speciality, little flasks of eau de cologne. No one came into the room, but from her bed, she could hear footsteps stop at the door, hesitate, and a secret hand would leave a package on the landing. Every now and again, she would lose consciousness and forget that Harry wasn't with her; she would look around for him and call out his name, in vain. She imagined she was crying out and chasing him from room to room or through the streets. But the people who were looking after her heard only low groans, suppressed as if in shame, and words spoken in French that they couldn't understand.

She came round during the night. All she could see was a lamp covered in a green silk shawl; the rest of the room was plunged into darkness. She felt as if this was not the first time she had suffered this way, that she had already been stretched out in a bed like this, had already brought a child into the world. This impression was so strange, so bewildering that she raised herself up in the bed and placed a trembling hand on the pillow beside her.

'My child? . . . Where is my child?'

Someone moistened her lips and forehead with some cool water and for an instant, she recognised Rose Liebig. The two women looked at each other.

'Rose . . . where is his father now?' Ada asked suddenly, forcing herself to smile weakly. 'I know that he's thinking about me at this very moment.'

'Of course,' murmured Rose, with pity. 'Of course.'

And she walked away, disappearing into the dark part of the room, leaving Ada alone with her ghosts; they rose up from every corner of the room: Aunt Raissa and Madame Mimi, Ben and Laurence. Only Harry was missing, and Ada felt as if her heart were being torn apart. Finally, the pain subsided, but the child still had not been born. Some of the older women walked quietly over to the bed. They wanted Ada to eat an orange; she sucked on a few sections of the fruit they had rolled in sugar and felt better, stronger. Everyone was talking all around her; they were listing the people who had died the previous evening during the uprising at the large factories in the southern suburbs.

'What a terrible time for a child to be born . . .' someone sighed. 'And the woman all on her own.'

'Nonsense!' said Rose. 'The most wealthy, the most cherished woman in the world feels all alone on the day when she brings her first child into the world, just as alone as a woman who is dying or the first woman ever to give birth.'

Was that really Rose Liebig who was talking? Or was Ada listening to a voice from within herself, wiser and older than herself, a voice that had so often consoled her in the past? She shifted in the big bed and the familiar, monotonous voices soothed her once more.

'I've heard there are still some places left for immigrants in Canada. I heard it from the sister of the Persian consul who knows the secretary of the owner of . . .'

Ada closed her eyes. Where had she heard that before? It was in Paris, in another world, centuries before. Everything was becoming confused, slipping away, disappearing. Had she really even known Harry? Or was it a dream? She shuddered for a moment at the idea that she might wake up as a child in her bedroom in the Ukraine and realise that she had imagined all those years of happiness and pain.

'And so,' she thought, 'I regret nothing. I have been happy. I may not have known it, but I have been unbelievably happy. I have been loved. I am still loved. I know that's true, in spite of the distance between us, in spite of the separation. And I still have my eyes and my hands and my wonderful work.'

She didn't think about the child. In the hours just before birth, the child is forgotten. Other people think about him, but not the suffering mother. Every so often, Ada wondered, 'But why am I in so much pain? My God, will it never end?'

The worst moment came as night was ending, the moment when the pain seems unbearable and the fear of death is strong. Ada feared it more than anyone: what would happen to her child?

She suddenly thought of Nastasia, as she had been long ago, and called out for help from that other little Jewish woman who had fled from country to country carrying her precious burden inside her.

The child came into the world and began to cry.

Ada could hear the noise from the marketplace: joyful sounds rose up to her room. It was a beautiful day with almost no snow or wind. They pushed Ada's bed over to the window, into the light, and tucked the baby in bed beside her. Everyone went away. Rose Liebig was sitting in a corner of the room, sewing. Just as you rest in the evening after walking all day long, just as your skin soaks up the coolness of the sheets, the softness of the bed after a day in the heat and dust, so Ada, eyes closed, felt a sense of physical, almost primal happiness sweep through her body, a feeling that was more wonderful than anything she had ever felt. Weakly, she moved her hand along the sheets and the feel of them filled her with sweet, peaceful joy. She watched the light against the windowpanes and smiled. She felt as if her body had been torn apart by pain and was not yet whole again, not yet able to resume her terrifying capacity to suffer when part of her body or soul was suffering. It had been liberated from its bondage: she was split into a thousand Adas, and each one of them was free, each one rejoiced with not a thought for the others, with not a thought, most importantly, for the real Ada and her past. Had she actually had a past? She had given up a part of her life for her newborn child, but he was giving her a wonderful gift; he shared his own riches with his mother: the gift of sleep, the gift of innocence, perhaps even the gift of forgetfulness.

The child was asleep in her arms; together they dozed off and woke up: the baby to cry, and Ada to smile as she looked at him.

He had fine dark hair and a large forehead. He didn't look like anyone in particular. She studied him intently but could find no features she recognised, yet, at the same time, he seemed very old and very wise, as all babies do when they are first born.

With deep astonishment and extraordinary joy, she could feel a faint, rapid rhythm beside her, the gentle beating of a heart that gave her two hearts. She thought of Harry then, when he lay in her arms. But Harry seemed far away; he had returned to his place in her dreams. He had been hers, and she had lost him. Her destiny was certainly harsh and incomprehensible, yet without quite knowing why, she sensed that she was at the brink of an explanation, of some truth that would suddenly shed light on the injustice of it all and resolve the dilemma. She had no doubt that her child knew something of this truth – and this is what made him look so old and wise; she knew the other part, she who had given up struggling, who asked for nothing, regretted nothing, she who felt so weary and carefree, both at the same time. Perhaps the two parts of this truth would merge to form a brilliant light? Fire destroys one tree after the other, until the entire forest is ablaze.

Like a child listing all the precious things he owns, she counted on her fingers: 'Painting, the baby, courage: with those things, you can live. You can live a good life.'

Rose Liebig was a little frightened by her silence; she stood up and looked over at the bed.

'Are you two all right?' she asked.

'We're fine,' said Ada.

She said it again and smiled: 'we' . . . For the first time in her life, she realised she could say this word and know for sure that it was true. And how sweet was its sound.

INTRODUCTION TO
THE FRENCH EDITION

Irène Némirovsky was born in Kiev on 11 February 1903. She was raised by a French governess, and spoke only French with her mother, with whom she had a difficult relationship (reflected in several of her novels). Her father was an important banker. When the October Revolution of 1917 broke out, a price was placed on his head, forcing him to go into hiding in Moscow with his family. It was at this time that Irène, for whom French had become as much her maternal language as Russian, discovered the short stories of de Maupassant, J.K. Huysmans's *À Rebours* (*Against the Grain*) and Oscar Wilde's *The Portrait of Dorian Gray*. The Némirovskys managed to flee to Finland; they then spent a year in Stockholm before settling in Paris in 1919, where her father managed to rebuild his fortune.

In 1929, after graduating in literature, Irène published her first novel, *David Golder*, which was greeted with unanimous critical acclaim. During the 1930s, she would publish nine novels and a collection of short stories: *Le Bal* (*The Ball*), *Le Malentendu* (*The Misunderstanding*), *Les Mouches d'automne* (published in English as *Snow in Autumn*), *L'Affaire Courilof* (*The Courilof Affair*), *Films parlés* (*Spoken films*), *Le Pion sur l'échequier* (*The Pawn on the*

Chessboard), *Le Vin de solitude* (*The Wine of Solitude*), *Jézabel* (*Jezebel*), *La Proie* (*The Prey*) and *Deux* (*Two*). *Les Chiens et les Loups* (*The Dogs and the Wolves*) was published in 1940. While taking refuge in the Saône-et-Loire region during the war, she wrote three books that would be published posthumously: *La Vie de Tchekhov* (*The Life of Chekhov*), 1946, *Les Biens de ce monde* (*All Our Worldly Goods*), 1947 and *Les Feux de l'automne* (*Autumn Fires*), 1957. While in the process of writing an ambitious novel opening with the exodus from Paris in June 1940, she was arrested in July 1942, sent to a transit camp at Pithiviers, then deported to Auschwitz, where she died in August 1942.

After her death, the Albin Michel Publishing House and Robert Esménard took responsibility for educating her two daughters, who had spent the rest of the war in hiding with their governess. They had been entrusted with their mother's last notebook, which contained the first two parts of the novel *Suite Française*, published in the autumn of 2004.

www.vintage-books.co.uk